Brain Cheese Buffet

Brain Cheese Buffet

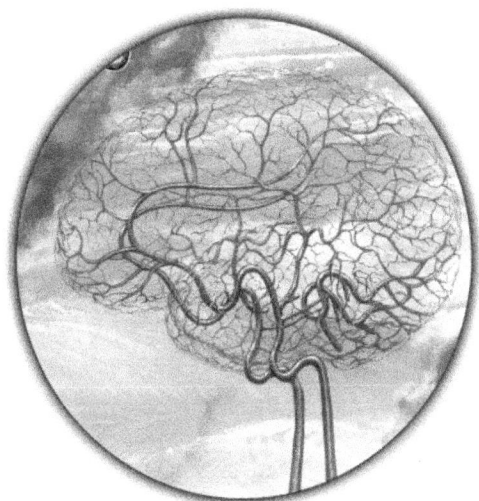

EDWARD LEE

deadite
press

DEADITE PRESS
205 NE BRYANT
PORTLAND, OR 97211

AN ERASERHEAD PRESS COMPANY
WWW.ERASERHEADPRESS.COM

ISBN: 1-936383-03-9

CONTENTS

Mr. Torso

Ol' Lud knew he was givin' 'em purpose by what he was doin'. This was God's work according ta the books he'd read, and Lud believed it might fierce, he did. *Yessiree,* he thought. *That's gettin' it.* He gandered cockeyed down at Miss August outa *Hustler.* As purdy a blondie as he'd ever seen. *Ooh, yeah.* Awright, so sometimes it took awhiles. Sometimes he had trouble gettin' the ol' crane ta rise, but jimmy Christmas, at sixty-one, what fella wouldn't, ya know?

What'd these gals be doin' otherwise? *Gettin' diseases an' all, smokin' the drugs, gettin' cornholed by fellas.* 'Stead Lud was helpin' 'em ta be what The Man Upstairs intended 'em ta be, an' givin' ta those without what they'se wanted fierce. And acorse paid fer. Ya know?

Lud's mitt needed ta jack hisself up a tad longer 'fore he'd be able to get it, so's he stared on at Miss August, one mighty purdy splittail with that velvety lookin' snatch on her an' that dandy pair of ribmelons. Yessir!

But it wasn't that he was no preevert or nothin' by's doin' this everday. He was puttin' some real meanin' in these gal's lives, just like the books said. He was givin' 'em purpose.

Once he was able ta pull hisself a stiffer an' get to it, he wondered what the gal in the August centerfold'd look like without any arms n' legs on her. *Problee not too good,* he reckoned.

But acorse sometimes God's work weren't purdy.

Tipps was contemplating the tenets of didactic Solipsism and its converse ideologies when he disembarked from his county car. *Positive teleology?* Tipps didn't buy it. It had to be subjectively existential. *It has to be*, he thought. *Any alternative is folly.*

County Technical Services looked like scarlet phantoms roving the darkness. Sirchie portable UV lamps glowed eerily purple. The techs wore red polyester utilities so that any accidental fiber fall wouldn't be confused as crime-scene residue by the Hair & Fibers crew back at Evidence Section. But Tipps, in his heather-gray Brooks Brothers suit, already harbored a clear notion that TSD was wasting their time.

The moon shone like a pallid face above the cornfield. Tipps walked toward the ravine, where red and blue lights throbbed. Maybe, by now, these south county boys were getting used to it. A young sergeant rested on one knee with his face in his hands.

"Get up," Tipps ordered. "You're not a creamcake, you're a county police officer. Start acting like it."

The kid stood up and blinked hard.

"Another 64?" Tipps asked.

"Yes sir. It's another torso thing."

Mr. Torso, Tipps thought. That's what he'd come to think of the perp as. Fifteen sets of limbs dumped on county roads like this the past three years. And three torsos, all, white cauc feems. The perp yanked their teeth and did an acid job on their faces, hands, and feet. Tipps ordered up the new g/p runs on all the parts but thus far to no avail. K-Y jelly and sperm in the three torsos; the sperm typed A-pos. *Big deal*, Tipps thought.

"Down there, sir." The cop pointed into the lit ravine. "I sorry, I just can't hack it."

This is getting to be a hard county, Tipps told himself and descended toward TSD's lights. Techs crawled on hands and knees with flash-hats. Field spots had been erected; they were looking for tire indentations to cast. "Mr. Torso strikes again," Tipps muttered when he glanced further. At the culvert, two more techs were pulling severed arms and legs out of the pipe. Then a figure seemed to drift out of the eerie light. Beck, the TSD field chief.

"So we got another torso job," Tipps said more than asked.

Beck, a woman, had thick glasses and frizzy black hair like a witch's. "Uh—huh," she replied. "Two arms, two legs. And another torso that doesn't match with the limbs. What's that total now? Four torsos?"

"Yeah," Tipps said. The torso lay off to the side, white slack breasts descending into its armpits. The stumps, like the others, looked healed over. The face was an acid scab.

"I'll know more once I get her in the shop, but I'm sure it's just like the others."

The others, Tipps reflected. The previous torsos had been crudely lobotomized, according to the deputy M.E. A hard pointed instrument thrust up through the left anterior eye socket. Eardrums punctured. Eyes glued shut. Mr. Torso was shutting down their senses. *Why?* Tipps wondered. "Do another g/p run," he said.

Beck half-smiled. "That's been a waste so far, Lieutenant. We're never gonna get a records match on a genetic profile."

"Just do it," Tipps said.

Beck's sarcasm dissolved when she looked again to the ravine. "It's just so macabre. This is the sixteenth set of limbs he's dumped but only the fourth body. What the fuck is he doing with bodies?"

Tipps saw her point. *And what in God's name*, he thought, *is the purpose behind all this?* Tipps felt strangely assured of that. His philosophies itched. He knew there was a purpose.

Ol' Lud's purpose, acorse, was ta get the gals knocked up. Then he'd wait till they dropped their rugrat an' he'd sell it ta folks who couldn't have critters of their own. An' he wasn't profiteerin' neither--he'd use the green ta pay the bills and give the leftover ta charity. Nothin' wrong with that.

Acorse he had ta do the job on the gals first. Seemed only proper an' humane like, to relieve 'em of the mental turmoil. An' he'd cut off their arms an' gams so's they could get by on less viddles and so's he wouldn't hafta worry 'bout 'em gettin' away. Ol' Lud poked their ears 'cos it didn't seem right fer their jiggled brains ta be hearin' things an' gettin' all confused, and same fer gluin' up their eyes. These gals didn't need ta be seein' stuff.

And 'cos he felt for 'em, he jiggled up their brains a tad just like the way his daddy'd do years ago when some of the cows an' hogs got too feisty. See, all ya do is stick the carvin' awl up under a gal's eye socket till ya hear the bone break, then ya give the awl a quick jiggle. Wouldn't kill 'em, just messed up their brains so they couldn't think. "'Botomized 'em," daddy called it. Lud didn't need fer the gals ta be thinkin' things an' all. That'd be cruel seein' that they couldn't see or hear no how, an' couldn't walk no more or pick stuff up. Acorse, he had ta be careful doin' the jiggle. See, a coupla gals kicked on him after awhiles, so's that's why Lud always disinfected the scratch awl now, so's no bad germs'd get up in their noggins. Yessir, Lud felt mighty bad about the four that died, but what could he do, ya know?

So he dumped 'em. Yanked out their pearly whites with a track wrench, an' burned up their kissers so's the cops couldn't recanize 'em and maybe figure out how he was nabbin' 'em.

Lud had 'em all rowed up in the basement, twelve of 'em. He'd lay each of 'em in a pig trough with one end cut out so's their lower parts'd kinda hang out over the edge. That ways all Lud had ta do was drop his drawers standin' right there when he gave 'em some peter and they could whiz an' poop without makin' a mess of thereselfs 'cuz Lud kept a milk bucket under each trough. He fed the gals three squares daily, good potatomash an' milk an' heathly stews 'cos he wanted nice *strong* critters ta sell. An' the gals could swaller 'n chew just fine 'cos Lud didn't pull their choppers unless they up an' croaked on him on account he seed on CNN one night 'bout how the coppers could 'denify dead folks by comparin' their teeth with dental records and some such.

Lud's routine was monthly. That's why he had twelve gals, ya know, one fer each month. Fer instance, right now it was August, so that's why he this very second had his peter in the August gal. He'd give it to her 'least three times a day, ever day fer the whole month. That way it'd stand ta reason she'd be good an' preggered by the time September rolled around. Then acorse he'd start givin it to the gal in the September trough. An' when he wasn't dickin' em, or gettin' 'em viddles or washin' 'em up, he'd go upstairs and check out the city paper classified fer folks lookin' fer a critter to 'dopt. Lot of them folks was rich and they'd pay good scratch with no questions asked rather'n wait a coupla years ta get a critter legal like through the 'doption agencies. An' in his spare time, Lud'd kick back an' read his favorite books 'bout the meanin' of life an' all. He liked those books just fine, he did.

Only problem was the task of gettin' it on with the gals. See, sometimes it took awhiles ta get his peter hard enough ta give 'em a good pokin' on account it was no easy thing fer *any* fella keep a stiffer when the gal was, like, ya know, didn't have no arms or gams. An' worse was the noises they made sometimes while Lud was tryin' ta get his nut, kinda mewlin' noises an' another noise like "gaaaaaa— gaaaaaaaa" on account of 'cos Lud had jiggled their brains. Yessiree, downright unappealin' they was ta look at an' listen to which is why ol' Lud'd put one of the girlie center-folds on their bellies so's he had somethin' inspirin' ta look at whiles he was givin' 'em the wood.

Lotta times too he'd go limp right in 'em an' pop out, like right now with this red hairt gal in the August trough. "Dag dabbit!" he cursed 'cos Lud, see, he never took the Lord's name in vain. Couldn't get a nut out noways like that! So poor Lud stepped back from the trough with his pants around his ankles so's he could jack hisself back up but meantimes the K-Y in the gal's babyhole'd get gummy. See, 'fore Lud got ta dickin' a gal he'd have ta give them a squirt of the K-Y on account the gals couldn't get wet no more thereself 'cos of the brain-'jiggle he gave 'em. But like just was mentioned, see, that K-Y up there'd go gummy sometimes just like right now with this red-hairt gal, so's Lud'd have ta kneel down an' hock a lunger right smackdab on her snatch ta wet her up again, all the whiles he's jackin' his peter. It got a right frustratin' sometimes. "Ain't got all blammed day ta be beatin' my peter 'front of a torso!" he hollered aloud. "Jiminy Christmas! Can't keep a good stiffer, can't hardly come no more!" Acorse when such things happened ta cause Lud ta pitch a fit, he'd let hisself calm down and get ta thinkin'. Shore, it weren't easy sometimes, but this was God's work. He oughta be grateful—lotta fellas his age couldn't get a stiffer at all no more and they'se shore as heck couldn't have out with a nut. The books made it clear ta him. It was The Man Upstairs Hisself who'd called on him ta do this deed an' by golly there weren't no way he was gonna fail The Man Upstairs! His work weren't always easy, weren't supposed ta be.

So Lud gandered down real hard at that girlie centerfold of Miss August, pretendin' it was her in that there trough 'stead of this red-hairt gal with no arms or gams goin' "gaaaaa—gaaaaaa!" an' he was jackin' hisself real hard an' fast eyein' them purdy centerfold hooters and that nice paper cooze an—"Yeah, lordy!" he celebrated 'cos there his peter went finally gettin' hard again. "Yeah, oh yeah! Here she comes, August!" he promised an' just as ol' Lud'd have his nut he stuck his peter back inta that stump sided red-hairt snatch an' got a good load of his dicksnot right up theres in her baby-makin' parts.

"Gaaaaa! Gaaaaaaaa!" went the gal's droolin' mouth.

"Yer quite welcome, missy," Lud replied.

Next morning Tipps' Guccis took him up to the city-district squad room where some newbies from south county vice swapped jokes.

"Hey, how's a torso play basketball?"

"How?"

"With difficulty!"

"Hey, guys, you know where a torso sleeps?"

"Where?"

"In a *trunk!*"

The explosion of laughter ceased when Tipps' shadow crossed the squad room floor. "Next guy I hear telling torso jokes gets transferred to district impound," was all he remarked, then moved to his office.

The sun in the window blinded him. Tipps didn't want the answers most cops wanted—he didn't give a shit. He didn't even care about justice. *Justice is only what the actualized self makes it*, he reflected. Tipps was obsessed with philosophy. He was forty-one, never married, had no friends. Nobody liked him, and he didn't like anybody, and that was the only aspect of his exterior life that he liked. He hated cops as much as he hated bad guys. He hated niggers, spics, slant-eyes. He hated pedophile rings and church coteries. He hated God and Satan and atheists, faith and disbelief, yuppies and bikers, homos, lezzies, the erotopathic and the celibate. He hated kikes, wops, and wasps. Especially wasps because he himself was born a wasp. He hated everybody and everything, because, somehow the nihilistic acknowledgment was all that kept him from feeling totally false. He hated falsehood.

He loved truth, and the philosophical calculations thereof. Truth, he believed, could only be derived via the self-assessment of the individual. For instance, there was no global *truth*. There was no political or societal *verity*. Only the truth of the separate individual against the terrascape of the universe. That's why Tipps had become a cop, because, further, it seemed that real truth could only be decrypted through the revelations of *purpose*, and such purpose was more thoroughly bared in the *spiritual* proximity to stress. Being a cop got him closer to the face that was the answer.

Fuck, he mused at his desk. He wanted to know the *purpose* of things, for it was the only way he'd ever discover *his* purpose. That's why the Mr. Torso case fascinated him. *If truth can only be defined on an individual stratum via one's conception of universal purpose, then what purpose is this? Tell me, Mr. Torso.*

It had to be unique. It had to be—

Brilliant, he considered. Mr. Torso was making effective efforts to avoid detection, which meant he was not pathological nor bipolar. The m.o. was identical, painstakingly so. Nor was Mr. Torso retrograde, schizoaffective, ritualized, or hallucinotic; if he were, the psych unit would've discerned that by now, and so would the Technical Services Division. *Mr. Torso,* Tipps thought. What purpose could there be behind the acts of such a man?

Tell me, Mr. Torso.

Tipps had to know.

Lud always 'ranged ta meet 'em out in the boonies, with phony plates on his pickup. Old lots, convenience stores an' the like.

"Oh thank God I can't believe it's true," yammered the blueblood lady when ol' Lud passed her the fresh, new critter. The critter made cute goo-goo sounds, its pudgy little brand-spankin' new fingers playin' with his new mommy's pearl necklace. She was crying she was so et up with happy. "Richard, give him the money."

Lud scratched his crotch sittin' back there in the back seat of this fancified big lux seedan, one of them 'spensive kraut cars was what he thought. But the gray hairt guy in the suit gave Lud a bad look. Then, kinda hezzatatin' an' twitchy, this fella asked, "Could you, uh, tell us a little bit about the mother?"

She's a torso, ya dipstick, Lud thought. *An' it was my spunk preggered her up. But what'choo care anyways? I got'cha what ya wanted, ain't I? Jiminy Christmas, these rich folks!*

"I mean," the suit said, "you're certain that this arrangement is consentual? I mean, the child wasn't . . . abducted or kidnaped or anything like that, right?"

"No way this critter here's kitnapped, mister, so's you's got nothin' to worry about." Then Lud felt the fella could use a reminder.

"Acorse, no questions asked is what we agreet, weren't it? Like ya said in yer ad, conferdential. Now if yawl gots second thoughts, that's fine too. I'lls just take the little critter back and yawl can sign back up at the 'doption agency, 'acorse if ya don't mind waitin' like five er six years."

"*Give him the money, Richard,*" the lady had out in a tone'a voice like the devil on a bad day. Women shore did have them some wrath now an' again. "*Give him the money so we can take our baby home! And I mean right now, Richard, *right now!*"

"Er, yes," mouthed the new papa in the suit. "Yes, of course." And then he passed ol' Lud an envelope full 'o hunnert' dollar bills stuffed like ta the tune of twenty grand. Lud shot the folks a smile. "I just knows in my heart that yawl'll raise yer new critter fines an' proper. Don't ferget ta teach 'im ta say his prayers ever night, an' make shore he's raised in the ways of The Man Upstairs now, ya hear?"

"We will," said the suit. "Thank you."

"Thank you thank you!" gushed the new mommy all silly-face happy and teary eyed. "You've made us very happy."

"Don't'chall thanks me 's much as The Man Upstairs," Lud said an' scooted outa the big lux kraut seedan parked at the QWIK-STOP. *'Cos it's Him that called me ta do this.* After the rich folks left, Lud hisself drove off in his beat-ta-holy-hail pickup, thinkin'. He had work ta do tonight. What with that skinny-ass brownyhead dyin' on him yesterday (Lud figured she musta got some bad germs up in her noggin when he jigged her brain, and that's why she didn't live long). He had to swipe hisself a new gal an' get her torsoed up 'cos the June trough was empty now. Acorse, 'fore he did that he figured he best git home ta that red-hairt August gal ta lay some afternoon peter on her, get some *good* spunk up her hole. After all, Lud had future orders now, and it didn't seem fit ta hafta keep God's work waitin'. An' he also knew, from his fave-urt books, that The Man Upstairs kept his mitts off the world itself, ever since Eve put her choppers ta that apple, so's there was physerolegy in play too, which was why ol' Lud knew he hadda get his dicksnot up the girl's hole many times a day as he could manage so's she'd be shore ta get preggered up just fine.

And bring new life unto the world.

Tipps wore the morgue's ghastly fluorescent light like a pallor; he could've passed for a well-dressed corpse himself, here in such company. Jan Beck, the TSD field chief, set a bottle of Snapple Raspberry Iced Tea on a Vision Series II blood-gas analyzer. "Be with you in a minute, sir," she offered, matching source-spectrums to the field indexes. Tipps wondered how she applied her own notions of truth to her overall assessment of human purpose. Did she *have* such an assessment? She histologized brains for a living, autopsied children, and had probably seen more guts than a fishmarket dumpster. *What is your truth?* he wondered.

"Your man wears size-11 shoes."

"That's great!" Tipps celebrated.

"Ground was wet last night." Beck chewed the end of a fat camel's-hair brush. "Left good impressions for the field boys." Rather despondently then, she closed a big red book entitled: *Pre-1980 U.S. Automotive Paint Index.* "I checked every source index we got, and it's not here."

"What's not here?" Tipps queried.

"Oh, I forgot to tell you. When he backed up to the ravine last night, his right-rear fender scraped the culvert rim. I ran the paint-residuum through the mass-photospectrometer. It's not stock-auto paint so I can't give you a make and model. All I can tell you is he drives a red vehicle."

Tipps felt delighted. Finally they had a real lead…

Beck continued, sipping her Snapple. "And that g/p-run you asked for? Well, you hit pay-dirt this time, Lieutenant. We got a positive match with the state CID records index. Torso Number Four has a name. Susan H. Bilkens."

"Why the hell's she got a genetic-profile record?"

"She's a whore, er, was. Six busts, five city, one county. Pressed charges against her first pimp last year so the city asked for a g/p-material sample. The pimp cut her up a little, they hoped the g/p-sample would match blood on the pimp's clothes." Beck let out a humorless chuckle. "Too bad it didn't wash in court, fuckin' judges must be out of their minds. But at least it gave the girl's name for a rundown."

"Susan H. Bilkens," Tipps repeated. He appraised the naked torso on the stainless-steel morgue platform which came complete with removable drain-trap and motorized height-adjustment. The torso's acid-burned face more resembled a mound of excrement, and her y-section had been stitched back up like a macabre zipper. "You said she's a hooker?"

"*Was* a hooker, that's right." Another chuckle. "She's just a dead torso now. Worked the West Street Block, the dope bars, till she shitnamed herself with the pimp thing. For the last year she was turning her tricks at a truck stop up on the Route."

"This is . . . *wonderful*," Tipps intoned.

"The postmortum gave us more of the same. Teeth manually extracted shortly after death. Eardrums ruptured, eyes glued shut with cyanoacrilate aka Wonder Glue. Minor insult across the lateral sulcus in the frontal lobe. He lobotomized her just like the others. Oh, and I was able to match her body with the arms and legs we found in Davidsonville four months ago. You ready for the bombshell?"

Tipps looked at her.

"Tally this up, Lieutenant. Like I said, we found her arms and legs *four months* ago."

"I heard you."

Beck sipped her Snapple. "When she died she was *two months* pregnant."

16

Two month's pregnant, he recited, motoring down Route 154 in his unmarked. It seemed spectacularly . . . hideous. With each revelation, Tipps felt beckoned to unveil Mr. Torso's conception of human truth, and, hence, his empirical purpose.

Mr. Torso, Tipps thought. *I'm going to get you, buddy, and I'm going to find out.*

Not only was Tipps a conclusionary-didactic nihilist, he was also a proficient investigator. A records check dropped the prostitute's life into his lap. Twenty-five years old, Caucasian, brown hair, brown eyes, 5'5", 121 pounds. Tipps wondered how much she weighed *without* her arms and legs. Since she had been run off the red-light block in town, she worked a truck stop near the county line called The Bonfire. Truck stops were the first places banished prostitutes fled to, and there was only one in all of south county . . .

He parked between two Peterbilt semi's at the end of the lot. The little dive of a restaurant glowed beyond, peppered with minute movement in its plate-glass windows. Tipps sung a tune in his mind, with a slight lyrical modification—"Eighteen Wheels And A Dozen Torsos"—scanning the Bonfire with a small pair of Bushnell 7x50's. In the binocular's infinity-shaped field, he could see them in there: Unkept, nutritionally depleted, desperate. Most, he knew, were clinical drug addicts, their only human purpose in the universe being to cater to the axiomatic and primordial male sex-drive in exchange for crack money. They fluttered about the restaurant interior, fussing with corpulent truck drivers whose stout arms provided tattoo-tapestries. Some of the girls dawdled outside, hidden within the gulf of shadows.

Tipps wondered about them, these sex-specters. Did they even realize their place in the ethereal universe? Did they ever ponder such considerations as existential verity, psycho-societal atomism, tripartite eudaemonistic thesis? *Do they ever wonder what their purpose is?* Tipps wondered to himself. *Do they even* have *a purpose?*

At once, Tipps sat up. The Bushnell's fine German optics easily revealed the dilapidated red pickup truck that pulled into the lot, as well as the long fresh scratch along the right-rear fender.

Lud loped outa the Bonfire, wearin' the usual overalls an' size-11 steel toes, totin' a bag of mags. See, the Bonfire up 'fore the register had thereselfs a rack of the girlie mags and a lotta the September issues'd just come out. Lud never quite reckoned why, for instance, the September mags always come out third week of August, not that he much cared. Next week'd be time ta start gettin' his peter up inta that lil' blondie with the hairlip sittin' cozy an' limbless in the September trough. She had a nice set of milk wagons on her but a joyhole big enough ta take a ham hock. What'd fellas been stickin up this gal ta get her so stretched out—their blammed heads? Or was she just born that way? Acorse bein' real big likes that'd make it easier for her ta drop critters-Jiminy, big as she was she could problee drop a whole kindergarten at once! An' the lips 'round her snatch looked like a bunch of hangin' lunchmeat er somethin'. 'Least she didn't make a ruckus like the gal in the August trough who Lud was gettin' a might sick of by now. See, that's why Lud buyed hisself new mags each month, ta open the centerfolds onta their bellies so's he could get his peter up proper an' come. An' on account of the June gal up an' dyin' on him an' his havin' ta dump her last night, Lud needed hisself a new gal ta take her place. These hookers always hanged out at the Bonfire 'cos the truckers was forever tryin' ta get their peters off in some splittail 'tween their long hauls, and ways it was set up, that big tookus-lot with all them semirigs parked alls over, Lud could propersition a gal right quick and have her outa there without no one bein' the wiser.

Walkin' down, though, he sawed all them rubbers layin' on the cement, like a whole lot of 'em, an' this made Lud right sad. *Don't fellas know nothin' these days?* Didn't fellas ever use their brains fer more'n skull-filler? The dicksnot, see, was fer more an just feelin' good whiles it was comm' out'cher peter. It's a 'lixer of life, it was. It was a special gift The Man Upstairs gave ta fellas so's they'se could have their peters in gals proper the way He intended an' get ta makin' critters once that good spunk got up there inna gal's baby-makin' parts. Givin' life an' all, that's what the dicksnot were all's about, see? Droppin' new rugrats onto the earth ta carry on with things the way God wanted. And it was a blammed shame seein' all's this good spunk wasted just fer the sake o' havin' a nut. Weren't supposed ta be shot inta some infernal conderm! These little things layin' all over lot, they was like a slap ta the face of The Man Upstairs in a way of reckonin', a way mankind'd figured on cheatin' the ways things was supposed t' be. Lud had a mind ta collect up all these rubbers each night an' empty 'em like maybe inta a soup bowl er somethin', them git hisself a turkey baster so's he could give each of his gals good squirt without havin' ta do it hisself. Acorse, that might not be such a hot idea considerin' all the devil-made diseases goin' 'round these days. Just seemed a cryin' shame fellas'd see fit to wastin' their juice like that, kinda in a way of like puttin' a little bit of God in a bag an' flushin' Him down the crapper or throwin' Him down on some dirty trucker parkin' lot—

"Hey, pops, for twenty bucks I'll suck your cock so hard your balls'll slide out of your peehole."

Lud gandered this little stringbean who'd came outa the shadows. They'se was all mostly rack-skinny like this one an' all had there-selves lank straight hair on 'em an' mostly little-type hooters 'cept 'acorse fer his September gal with that big ol' pair of the chest melons. "Well, say there, missy, that sounds like a right deal ta me," Lud enthused "Just foller me yonder to my truck'n we'll have ourselfs a *dandy* ol' time"

They gots in the pickup an' Lud had his peter out even 'fore she could pussy-pocket that double-sawbuck he gave her. Then she opened her yap an' got ta work lickety-split. Lud figured he'd let her suck awhiles, not that he was plannin' ta waste a perfectly good load of his critter-goo on her yap but just ta let her get on it awhiles so's he'd be good'n boned up fer later when he were givin' his August gal her beddy-bye pop. Lud in fact 'preciated it. It made things easier later ta have his stiffer all hot'n bothered by a gal who still had her arms an' gams connected to her, yessir, right nice change ta be with somethin' other'n a, brain-jiggered blabberin' torso with a girlhole full of the K-Y. An' this little stringbean here was just a'smokin' his pole like a regler trooper she was, an' kindly givin' his ballbag a good feelup while she was goin'. *Lordy, can this gal suck a peter!* Lud exclaimed in thought. *A regler machine she is, like ta suck the peterskin right off my bone!* Then she stopped sucking a speck an' kinda snotty said, "Hey pops, I been doing this a while. You getting close?"

"Wells, try ta be patient, missy. Ol' fella the likes of me sometimes takes awhiles ta get his nut out."

She sucked awhiles more, harder an' faster with that little hand of hers just a pumpin' away on his sack like it were a full-up milkbag on a cow, an' she was a'slurpin' an' lickin' an really goin' t'town down there on his meat an' makin' more noise than a couple of thousand-pound Hampshire hogs havin' a row in the mudhole, but then she stops again an' bellyaches, "Come on, pops. Hurry up and come, will ya? I ain't got all night."

"What'choo *got*, missy," Lud kindly corrected, "is yer whole life ta turn from the errah of yer ways an' starts ta doin' what gals was meant ta do in the eyes of The Man Upstairs, like havin' critters and perpetcheratin' the species. What I'se talkin' 'bout, missy, is the purpose of the whole ball of wax we calls life," an' just right then lickety-split, Lud gave her a thunk fierce on the bean with a empty Carling bottle an' put her little lights right out. He stuffed her down inta the footwell an' droved outa the lot with his peter still out'n stickin' up all high an' mighty from that humdinger of a suck she were givin' him, an' it kinda seemed a shame, ya know, what he'd hafta be doin' ta her shortly.

Way he'd do it, see, is he'd take 'em downstairs an' make 'em swaller a bowl of potatomash full of horse trank, so they'd be out deep for a good spell. Then he'd glue up their eyes an' poke their ears an' 'botermize 'em with the scratch awl so's they wouldn't sense no more an' not be confused an' all. Then he'd lop off their arms and gams with his field adze, which were like a axe only the blade went crossways, and acorse before he'd do that he'd tie off each arm an' leg right close with heavy sisal rope so's the gals wouldn't bleed ta death once he had off with their limbs.

And that's just what Lud did when he gots back ta the house with that little suckjob gal he picked hisself up at the Bonfire. Each time looked a little neater, 'fact by now Ol' Lud could have off with a gal's arms an' gams just as neat'n clean as you'd ever want, provided acorse that you'd ever in the first place *want* a livin' torso in yer basement. The stumps'd heal over just fine in about a coupla weeks, then he'd be all set ta get ta pokin' her. This is one here, now that she were buck nekit, had some right nice little hooters on her an' a nice big clump a'hair down there on her babyhole, an' she even had a real fine little line'a hair goin' from her snatch ta her bellybutton which Lud always thought was just as cute as could be. One thing he didn't much care fer, though, was the tattoos—lotta these gals had tattoos on 'em—like this here brownyhead who sported one just over her right tittie, a silly little heart with a knife in it it looked like. Seemed a blammed shame ta Lud that gals'd have so little respect fer their bods ta scar 'em up like that 'cos the ways Lud saw it, 'least accordin' ta the books he'd read, was the body was a temple of The Man Upstairs and ta scar it up with silly tattoos were just the same as like throwin' garbage in a church or spraypaintin' the swear words on the altar an' bustin' up the stainglass winders with stones an' such. Didn't matter now, though, not fer this stringbean little brownyhead 'cos now she were well on her way ta some real godlylike meanin' in the scheme of life. Lud'd wait a spell 'for gettin' her settled down inta the June trough though, an' meantime, he bandaged up her stumps

21

so's she wouldn't get no 'nfections. Then he picked up her arms an' gams'n carried 'em upstairs ta put 'em in the truck fer dumpin' a little later after he burned up the hands 'n feet with mercuric acid, an' he's walkin up them stairs his size 11s goin' *clump clump clump* but, see, he stopped in his tracks on the top landin' 'cos first thing he sawwed was some fancified fella in a suit waitin' for him an' this fella had in his mitt a big tookus-gun that he was a'pointin' right smackdab at Lud's face . . .

"The blammed tarnations!" exclaimed the old man in overalls. He'd stopped cold on the landing, his arms heavy-laden with—

Limbs, Tipps realized. *He's carrying severed limbs.* "Don't move." Tipps stared at the wizened man, astonished. He kept a headshot bead in the adjustable sights of his Glock 17, whose clip was full of 9mm Remington hardball. His brain seemed to tick with arcane calculations. "Now," Tipps said. "Drop the . . . limbs."

The old man frowned, then released his burden. Two arms and two legs thunked to the hardwood floor.

"Sit down in that chair next to the highboy. Keep your hands in your lap. Fuck with me and I blow your goddamn head off."

Wincing, the old man seated himself in an antique cane chair that creaked with his weight. "Ain't no call fer swear words, son, and no call ta be takin' the Lord's name in vain."

Tipps kept the gun on him. "You're the guy . . . Mr. Torso."

"That what they'se callin' me?" Mr. Torso sputtered. "Blammed silliest-ass name I ever did hear."

But Tipps' thoughts revolved in a kaleidoscope of wonder, triumph, and conceit. *I got him*, he thought. *I got Mr. Torso.*

"You're a blammed copper, ain't'cha?" Lud asked. "How'd ya find me, son? Tells me that."

"I followed you from the truck stop."

Lud could'a smacked hisself right in the head. *I am just done ET UP with a case of the DUMBASS!* Led this poker-kisser copper in the fancified Ward an' Roebuck suit straight to him! *Jiminy Christmas I must'a passed my brain out my butthole last time I went ta the crapper!*

But, acorse . . .

Lud believed in proverdence. He believed what he eyeballed in them there books, an' he believed The Man Upstairs shore worked in some strange ways. An' it was proverdence he reckoned that this copper'd made him sit in the chair right next ta his dead mama's old highboy. And Lud knowed full well that in the top drawer was daddy's big ol' Webley revolver . . .

Tipps' gaze flicked about. It was an untold fantasy: *I'm in Mr. Torso's house!* "I want to know what you've been doing?"

"What'cha mean, son?"

"What do I mean?" Tipps could've laughed. "I want to know why you've dismembered sixteen women over the last three years, that's what I want to know. You're keeping them alive, aren't you?"

Mr. Torso's white hair stuck up in dishevelment, his chin studded with white whiskers. "Keepin' what alive?"

"The girls! The . . . torsos!" Tipps yelled. "My forensic tech told me the torso you dumped last night died within forty-eight hours, you crazy old asshole! We matched her body to a set of limbs you dumped four months ago, and she was *two months pregnant!* You're impregnating them, aren't you? Tell me why, goddamn it!"

Mr. Torso shut his eyes. "Aw, son, would ya *please* stop takin' tha Lord's name in vain? Come on, now."

Tipps took a step forward, training the Glock on the old man's 5x zone. But at that precise moment his flicking gaze snagged on a row of books atop the veneered highboy. *What the . . . hell?* Many of the titles he recognized, many he owned himself. The chief works of history's most preeminent philosophical minds. Sartre, Kant, Sophocles, and Hegel. Plato, Heidegger, and Jaspers. Aquinas, Kierkegaard . . .

23

"You . . .," Tipps faltered, "read . . . *this?*"

"Acorse," Mr. Torso affirmed. "What, just 'cos I wears overalls 'an live in the sticks, ya think I'se just some dumb-tookus rube with no hankerin' of the meanin' of life? Lemme tell ya somethin', son. I ain't no sexshool preevert like ya problee think. An' I'se ain't no psykerpath."

"What are you then?" Tipps' question grated like gravel.

Calmly, Mr. Torso went on, "I'se a perveyer of sorts, ya know? A perveyer of objectified human dynamics. Volunteeristic idealism's what they'se call it, son. See, the abserlute will is a irrational force 'less ya apply it ta the mechanistics of causal posertivity as a kinda counter-force ta the evil concreteness of neeherlistic doctrine. What I mean, son, is as indervividuals of the self-same unerverse, we'se all subject ta the metterphysical duality scape, and we must realize what we'se are as transcendental units of bein an' then engage ourselves with objectertive *acts*, son, ta turn the do-dads of our units of bein' into a functional deliverance of subjecterive posertivity in the ways of The Man Upstairs, see? No, I ain't no psykerpath. I'se a vassal, er a perpetcherater of Kierkegaardian fundermentals of human purpose."

Tipps stared as though he'd downed a fifth of Johnny Black in one chug. *Holy fucking shit!* he thought. *Mr. Torso . . . is a teleologic Christian phenomenalist!*

"It's takin' things inta our own mitts, see? Like with the gals, livin' in a neeherlistic void of spiritual vacuity. I do what I do ta give 'em the transertive *purpose* thats they'd never reckon on their own. I'se savin' 'em from the clutches of human abserlutism, son, ya know, savin' 'em from wastin' their potential as posertive units of bein'. All they'd be doin' otherwise is gettin' the AIDS, the herpes, gettin' abortions, smokin' the drugs, an' gettin' thereselfs problee beat up an' kilt. But alls forces in the universe is cyclic—like, ya know, one unit of bein' feedin' the other to a abserlute whole. Shore, I'se sells the critters but only ta folks who can't have none thereselfs no ways. An' the scratch I don't need ta keep good care of the gals, I gives to charity."

Tipps felt stupefied, locked in rigor. His astonishment caused the Glock's front sights to drift...

"It's all purpose, son. Human abserlute *purpose*.

Purpose, Tipps paused to wonder—

—and in that pause, a size 11 steel-toed boot socked up and caught Tipps square in the groin. He went down--the pain was incalculable. Through blurred and spider-cracked vision, he saw Mr. Torso standing now, rooting through the highboy's drawers.

"Daggit! Where's that big-tookus Webley!"

Tipps' gunhand trembled as he extended his arm. He managed to squeeze off a double-tap—*pap! pap!*—and somehow both 9mm bullets hit Mr. Torso between the legs, from behind—

"Holy Jesus Moses ta Pete!" the old man wailed, collapsing and clutching the bloodflow at his groin. "Ya blammed neeherlistic copper bastard! Ya done shot me in the *dickbag!"*

Tipps, still shuddering in his own pain, crawled forward to finish the job. He could scarcely breathe. But when he raised gun—

What the—

—his foe's crabbed hand slapped up and pushed it away, and at the same time a terrifying arc-movement fluttered overhead.

Then came a hideous *kaCRACK!*

Tipps' world blanked out like a power failure.

"Bet'cha got yerself a headache like a Old Crow hangover, huh?" A chuckle. Movement. "Yeah, I cracked ya a good one right smackdab on the bean with the butt of my daddy's big-tookus Webley .455. Took ya right out, it did."

When Tipps woke, he felt elevated somehow, drifting . . .

"Was all fired up ta kill ya but then I gots ta thinkin'."

To the right and left, Tipps saw a long row of what appeared to be open-ended metal troughs on stilts. Twelve troughs in all, each labeled by masking tape with a different consecutive month. Tipps throat swelled shut . . .

Each trough contained a torso.

"Say hello ta my gals, copper."

Each lay naked in their trough, their skin lean, white, and sweating in the basement's heat and incandescent glare. Healed-over stumped hips were visible at each trough-end. As the line of torsos progressed, Tipps couldn't help but note an increasing state of pregnancy: the later torsos sported bellies so distended they seemed on the verge of rupture, white skin stretched pin-prick tight against the burgeoning inner human freight. Fleshy navelbuds turned inside-out. Breasts heavy with mother's milk.

Immediately before him lay a wan torso with matted red hair. The slack face with sealed eyes twitched, the head lolled. "Gaaaa!" she said. "Gaaaaa!"

"This here's my August gal," Mr. Torso introduced. He stood at Tipps side. "Been spunkin' her up daily since the first of month so's ta git her good'n preggered."

"Gaaa! Gaaaaa!" she repeated.

"A regler chatterbox, ain't she? Blabbers like that on account I'se 'botermized her, ya know, jigged up her brain a tad so's she won't worry an' be confused an' such. Don't seem fair fer the gals ta keep their senses, bein' in such a state. S'why I glued up their eyes too, an' poked their ears. But don't 'cha worry none, 'cos all their baby-makin' parts works just fine."

Now Tipps deciphered the drifting sensation. His vision cleared further, and four shuddering glances showed him that he'd been divorced of all four limbs. His torso was suspended in a harness that hung from a hook over the trough. Eleven more such hooks were sunk into the ceiling rafter before each torso.

"Oh, I'se ain't gonna fiddle with *yer* eyes an' ears," Mr. Torso promised. "Nor's I gonna 'botermize ya either. See, a fella's sexshool responses are all up in his noggin, so's I can't be jiggin' yer brain like I'se done ta the gals. Can't very well git yerself a stiffer with yer brain all jigged up, now can ya?"

Tipps groaned from deep in his chest. He swayed ever-so-slightly.

"It's proverdence, son. Okay, shore, ya shot me right smack in the balls, but see, old as I am I was havin' a rough time keepin' the crane up anyways, and sometimes I'se just couldn't get a nut outa me ta save my life."

"What," came Tipps' desolate, parched whisper, "did you say about providence?"

"This, son. Me, you, the gals here—everthing. This is *God's* work, ya know, an' I figure that's why He sent ya to me, so's you can continue with His work. Keep up the human telerlogic cycle that proverdence ordained fer us. Ya know?"

Tipps' brain reeled. The hanging harness which satcheled him continued to sway ever-so-slightly. He saw that his butchered hips were exactly aligned with the redhead's stump-flanked vagina.

"Ain't much point at all ta life if we don't never comes ta realizin' our unerversal purpose . . ."

Tipps groaned again, swaying. The word, once ever-important to him, was now his haunting, his curse. And somehow, in spite of what had been done to him, and equally in spite of how he would spend the rest of his life, he managed to think: *You asked for it, Tipps, and now you got it. Purpose* .

"An' don't'cha worry none. That's why I'se here, son, ta help ya," said Mr. Torso as he opened the brand-new centerfold and carefully lay it on the redhead's belly.

Miss Torso

The woman had no arms; her name was Spooky, and the name suited her. Carbon-black hair and murky blue eyes, one iris minutely larger than the other due to a genetic defect called emmetropic binocular deviation. A demure, lilting voice but a mouth fouler than a waste hopper at a pork-processing plant. If anything, she was an interesting person—diverse and extraordinary. Spooky stood almost six feet tall, a hundred and twenty pounds, emaciated to near breastlessness, and all thin blue veins beneath parchment-white skin. It was the ice a.k.a. crank a.k.a. crystalized methamphetamine that kept her in the perpetual state of borderline starvation. Eleven years ago she'd been a runway model for the Ford Agency. A cover for *Allure* and *90's Woman,* a stint for Betsey Johnson, and several cosmetic commercials. After so many thousand-dollar-per-day shoots, however, it hadn't taken Spooky long to become utterly habituated to drugs. The fall was fast. When Vinchetti's spotters had seen her turning tricks in Utica, they'd snapped her right up; Vinchetti liked them tall, slim, and gutter-mouthed. One night she'd been higher than Robert Blake's attorney fees when she'd made the very grave mistake of attempting to seduce one of Vinchetti's most loyal buttons, Paulie, whose job it had been that evening to drive her home after her nightly visit to the compound; she'd confided: "Paulie, I fuckin' absolutely fuckin' *hate* fucking Vinch. He's got a little dick, and his breath could knock down a motherfuckin' brick wall," and this she related with her hand deftly plying Paulie's crotch. Paulie had simply smiled, shaking his head, and walked right back into the compound to relate the entirety of the incident to Vinchetti, who, by the way, was the supreme boss of what the U.S. Justice Department referred to as the Vinchetti/Lonna/ Stello Crime Pyramid. Vinchetti controlled virtually all of the white heroin and underground porn distribution on the east coast. At any rate, as recompense for this foolish slight, Vinchetti's personal doctor, a well-spoken, Deloreaneasque former Beverly Hills plastic surgeon named Winston F. Prouty, had painlessly amputated Spooky's arms two inches above the elbows. Now Vinchetti used her for kink tricks and videos. He wanted plenty of stump left on each arm, so that the stumps could be inserted into other women during four-and five-ways. It made for great footage.

"Camera ready?" Frankie asked.

Nick made a few adjustments on the tripod. "Just about."

"Lights bright enough, Nick?" Spooky complained in her velvet-soft voice. She sat upright, nude, on the very cheap coffee table that complemented the "suite," which was actually a room at the Howard Johnson's on Route 233 near Rome, New York. They got a special rate of ten dollars for two hours because the bathroom was completely out of order thanks to the crack dealers who'd trashed the place last week when a drop went bad. Nick and Frankie figured they'd spend the money they'd saved on extra drugs. This was a scat flick. Who needed a fuckin' bathroom?

"Fuckin' lights are cookin' me like a motherfuckin' curry-and-ginger pheasant satay," Spooky maintained her complaint, the simile prompted by old memories of four-star Big Apple cuisine back when she was with Ford.

"Live with it, bitch," Frankie remarked.

"Throat yourself, you dead-dick goombah motherfucker," Spooky quietly retorted.

"Jerk me off," Frankie snapped back. Then he paused and belted out a laugh. "Oh, wait a minute! You *can't* jerk me off! 'Cos you ain't got no *hands!*"

"Yeah, I *wish* I had hands, then I could give you the finger." She looked at Nick. "How do you like this useless piece of shit? Fuckin' guy's got more cock than *three* men and he can't do shit with the motherfucker. What good's a stunt-cock who can't fuck? Like tits on a motherfuckin' bull."

Frankie did not take these remarks particularly well. His paste-white prescription-morphine-derivative-junkie face pinkened at the insult. "You fuckin' armless jizz-can, I was the number one male porn star for a year!"

"Yeah, motherfucker, and what are you now? A dead-dick goombah motherfucker. Gonna take you all motherfuckin' night to get your dick half-hard like last time?"

Frankie stood naked and shuddering like Parkinson's, his once steroid-embellished muscles now sagging in debilitation. "Why, I oughta—"

Nick appeared weary. "Frankie, come on. We only got an hour left, and we gotta do a twenty-minute scat."

Spooky chuckled as she sat, kind of hunched over now. At her waistline, not a single roll of fat could be seen, as if her musculature had been coated with white wall paint. "Frankie's fuckin' nervous 'cos he knows he won't be able to fuckin' get it up, and if Frankie can't get it up, Vinch won't have any reason to keep him around any fuckin' more. This time next week he'll be in one of the fuckin' pylons on that new train bridge they're building across the Mohawk River. Smackheads can't get it up." Spooky grinned ever so subtly, batting her eyes. "Live with it."

Frankie was close to convulsions now. "I ain't no junkie!" he bellowed, needle tracks standing out like stitches on both arms.

Even Nick spared a chuckle at this one. "Frankie, face it. You're a junkie," he said as he lit his pipe and sucked down some crystal meth fumes. "So let's just get on with it. If you can't do the wet shot, I'll do it. Then you shit on her face at the end."

"Oh, not another one of those," Spooky said.

Frankie pointed his finger at her like a Beretta 92. "*Yes,* another one of those, whore. And I ate a whole plate of fried garlic and squid ravioli for lunch. Just for you."

Spooky did not look pleased but by now this was pretty much par for her personal golf course. She raised her stumps as if she actually had arms to throw up in concession. "So let's just do this motherfucker and get it the fuck over with."

"Good idea." Nick put down the pipe and was re-focusing on the coffee table. He was naked too, by the way, and nearly as emaciated as Frankie, yet not so well-endowed. At least his still worked, though, after a few Viagras which he popped a moment later. He passed the bottle to Frankie. "You're letting the chick psych you out. Here, and hurry it up. The Yankees are on."

Frankie, still pouting, popped half the bottle.

"Jesus, Frankie! You'll OD!" Nick yelled.

"God, I hope so," Spooky said.

"Just gimme a minute," Frankie said, assured. His dick was flaccid as a handful of overcooked spaghetti, *twelve inches* of overcooked spaghetti, to be more precise. At any rate, it was impressive. Like a fuckin' pork tenderloin between his legs.

Spooky needed no prompting when Nick put his crotch in front of her eerily still-pretty face. She sucked like the destitute, maladapted scat-junkie trooper that she was. Nick wasn't quite so far along in the drug-induced libidinal-system debilitation as Frankie. It only took him ten minutes to pull six inches of crane.

"I'm ready," he said. "How 'bout you?"

Frankie huffed, puffed-faced and masturbating as if working a bicycle pump to save his life. Soon, though, things south of the waistline began to inflate.

Spooky grinned. "Think harder about your dad, Frankie."

"FUCK!" Frankie bellowed. The image of his father—a man who'd beaten and sodomized Frankie from ages four through fourteen—couldn't have presented a less-erotic reaction in Frankie's mind. The mammoth penis went dead-flaccid in about a second.

Laughter fluttered from Spooky's throat, gentle as a stream of moths.

"Come on, Spooky," Nick reasoned. "Lay off him. You're fuckin' him up."

"I can't fuckin' help it. I hate that greaseball motherfucker. Doesn't fuckin' matter what I say any-fuckin'-way. It's gonna take that big lummox till next Easter to get half wood. He might as well be jerking off a fuckin' empty rubber."

Frankie's dead-meat cock flapped against his leg when he turned briskly and glared at Spooky. "I oughta—"

"You oughta *what?* Huh? I'll tell you what you *oughta* fuckin' do. You *oughta* grow a dick that works, you fuckin' pasta-scarfing piss-ant small-time mob errand-boy very-quickly-outliving-his-usefulness no-dick piece of garbage."

Frankie bulled forward, Nick pushing him back. "I oughta fuckin' kill you," Frankie yelled.

Spooky laughed, raising her stumps. "Shit, I've been begging for someone to kill me for ten motherfuckin' years." Her pair of diminutive tattoos enforced this assertion: rifle-scope crosshairs over her heart and, along the front of her throat, a six-inch perforation mark and the words CUT HERE. "You don't have the fuckin' balls to kill me, Frankie. There's nothing in your sack but two dead eggs."

Nick was fighting the losing battle in trying to push Frankie away from her. "Frankie, Frankie, come on, don't do it!" Nick yelled. "Vinch wants her alive for the scats–you kill her and we're *all* lunch meat."

"I don't care! I'm killin' her!"

"Did you blow your dad, or did he just fuck you in the ass, huh, Frankie?" Spooky continued to taunt. "Bet you got hard every time back then."

"I'm gonna kill her, Nick, I'm gonna—"

"You're an impotent waste of space, Frankie," she saw fit to add. "Do the human race a favor. Fuckin' hang yourself."

"You're dead, bitch! *Dead!*"

"Cool down, Frankie," Nick implored. "Cool down. You kill her, then Vinch'll have that psycho doctor of his do a job on both of us. You heard about what he did to Tony and Darcy, didn't you?"

Frankie stalled momentarily. It wasn't a pretty story. Indeed, then, he began to cool down.

A grateful impasse ensued. Frankie gained his composure. "All right, all right," he conceded. He stood feet apart, closed his eyes, and began to masturbate again. Spooky sighed, asked Nick, "Hey, load a pipe and light me up first, will you? I'm motherfuckin' feenin', like, really fuckin' bad." This was but one inconvenience of being armless: Spooky, a clinical drug addict, couldn't smoke drugs without assistance. Nor could she wipe her ass, effectively wash herself, clip her toenails, etc. "I've gotta have a hit. I got the motherfuckin' meth bugs crawling all over me. How about it, Nick?"

"No," Nick put his foot down. "When we're done."

"Fuck that motherfuckin' shit, man! I need some ice! Now!"

"When we're done," Nick repeated, half-blitzed himself.

"Come on, Nick. I'll stick my tongue up your asshole."

Nick frowned. Such favors he couldn't have been less interested in. All he wanted to do was ride his meth-buzz, get his cum-shot, and catch the Yankees. Clemens was pitching tonight, thank God.

"I need some batu, man! I need some fuckin' cristy! I'm not kidding."

"You'll have to wait. Maybe if you gotta wait, you won't fuck with Frankie's head anymore."

"Yeah," Frankie growled; the grin on his face denoted great pride. He turned around, displaying quite an achievement: twelve inches of very erect genitals. His eyes thinned ruefully at Spooky. "How's *that* for some dead dick, hose-bag?"

Spooky tossed a shoulder. "Hey, Frankie, when you were a baby, did you swallow your dad's nut, or spit?"

Frankie's grand twelve-incher went limp in an instant. "I'm gonna kill her!" he re-exploded, and this time Nick was off balance when he lunged to push Frankie away.

"My guess is you swallowed," Spooky conjectured, not even flinching as her ogre-sized nemesis struggled to reach her. "You look like a swallower. Bet your parents didn't even need to buy any baby food because of all that nut you were eating every day."

"Frankie–no!" Nick shouted, but—

SMACK!

Too late.

Frankie's primordial rage propelled his fist over Nick's shoulder where it connected with Spooky's chin effectively as a Tyson right-cross. Spooky's head snapped back, then her upper-body snapped back, all so fast she could only be seen as a chalk-white blur.

She lay perfectly still on the cheap coffee table.

Nick and Frankie gaped down, bug-eyed. They knew at a glance. Spooky's head hung over the table edge, her eyes crossed and wide open, her tongue hanging out. The silence was absolute.

"Man. Oh, man," Nick whispered. Beads of sweat wrung out of his pores. "Frankie, you better pray she ain't . . ." He couldn't even say the rest.

He knelt down, put an ear to her chest.

And gulped.

He felt around her neck for a pulse.

Gulped again.

Then he raged up at Frankie: "You big dumb cement-head motherfucker! You killed her!"

"I-I-I" Frankie gaped. "No, she—"

"Fuckbrain! You broke her neck against the edge of the table!"

"No, I-I-I . . ." Frankie was remiss for locution. "No. She fell, and her neck . . . It got broke."

"You KILLED THE BITCH! And now Vinchetti's gonna have

one of his crew KILL US! They'll hang us upside down by meat hooks through our assholes and blowtorch us! He'll have that crazy-ass doctor cut all our skin off!"

Frankie started to blubber he was so shit-scared. Nick sat dejected on the floor, head bowed.

"Let's-let's-let's just . . . leave town!" Frankie suggested. "Go somewhere. Hide."

"We could go to Mars and it wouldn't matter—Vinchetti would find us. We could go to fuckin' Egypt and bury ourselves a thousand feet under one of the pyramids and he would find us. We killed his best scat girl—Vinchetti *loves* scat. He'll be more pissed off about this than when the Yankees lost the series to Arizona."

"We're dead," Frankie blubbered.

Nick just nodded.

"Let's just-let's just-let's just—leave her here," came Frankie's next brilliant idea. "Just say she croaked, say she OD'd or somethin'. Yeah. Leave her here."

"It's a fuckin' Howard Johnsons! We can't leave a dead meth-head whore with no arms in a *Howard Johnsons!* You *murdered* her! Our prints are all over the room! The clerk saw us come in. This is a homicide scene, Einstein."

Frankie maintained his frantic blubbering. "Well-well-well let's dump her body. Dump her body in the canal. Then we can say some of Peroni's boys muscled her away from us. Peroni's been trying to horn in on Vinch's scat and nek market for years, and he's dumped a lot of bodies in the canal. The cops'd think it was Peroni."

Nick opened his mouth to voice further objection but—

"Hmm," he said.

"Vinch might believe it, Nick."

"He might. He just might." Nick glanced around, brain ticking. It was a bad plan but it was all they had. "Frankie, put your clothes back on. Then take the camera, lights, and tripods back out to the Caddy and put it all in the trunk." Now he was looking at the long suitcase they'd carried the equipment in. "We'll carry Spooky out in that."

"In what?" Frankie was stepping into his slacks. "You mean the suitcase?"

"Yeah. The suitcase."

Frankie scratched his chin. "Oh, Nick, I don't know. I don't think she'll fit."

Nick got up and grabbed his eight-inch Gerber Mk IV sheath knife off the dresser. "She'll fit just fine, Frankie. After I cut her legs off."

One time-saver was the plastic drop cloth they'd already spread out under the coffee table. This was, after all, a scat film scene. Never Leave A Mess was the rule. The trashed bathroom presented a bit of a problem, though, until Nick put the brain God gave him to work. The bathroom was padlocked shut—hence, no bath tub to cut her legs off in and, doubly hence, no place for all the blood to drain. Nick deftly cut four yard-long lengths of extension cord and began to apply the tourniquets just as they'd taught him in the Army. He cranked the first two on at the top of each thigh as close as possible to the hip joint, then two more a half-inch below the first two. He cranked them all down tight and tied them off. Next, with the Gerber, he began to cut. He cut all the way around each thigh, straight to the bone. Sharp as the Gerber was, the task proved much, much, much, much, much, much, much more difficult than one would think. Very little blood leaked out, however, due to the dual ligatures on each leg. A hammer and chisel from the Caddy's tool box neatly cracked each thigh bone—

And off the legs came.

"Nice job, Nick," Frankie complimented.

"Thanks."

Spooky's torso fit perfectly into the suitcase, and the legs went right on top. They zipped the suitcase up, slid it into the Caddy's back seat, discarded the drop cloth into the motel dumpster, and drove away.

Nick turned on the radio and smiled. What better harbinger could he ask for? The Yankees were beating Baltimore 11-1.

And it was only the fifth inning.

"I don't know about the canal, Frankie." Nick appraised the long stripe of black water from the road, trying to drive normally. "I saw two cops on the other side."

"They were just roosting," Frankie felt confident. "Eatin' donuts and reading the funny papers. They'll go back on patrol soon. Let's just kill some time, drive around a while."

"Frankie, we got a fuckin' torso in a suitcase in the back seat. I'd kind of like to get rid of it as soon as fuckin' possible, know what I mean?"

Frankie nodded, seeing the logic. "Fuck, you got any Demerol, Nick? I'm all out and I need a bang."

"Wait till we get back to the compound. And you better *pray* that Vinch believes our story 'cos if he don't you're gonna need a shitload of Demerol for when that kooky doctor starts doing the job on you."

"Fuck. I *definitely* need a hit."

Nick pulled a u-turn, a sudden endeavor occurring to him.

"Where we going now? Those cops ain't left the canal yet."

"The Kwik-Mart," Nick answered. "For Wet-Naps."

"Wet-Naps? We goin' for ribs?"

Nick frowned. "No, we ain't goin' for ribs. We—or, I mean *you*—gotta wipe down everything we touched." Nick pointed to his head. "Think, Frankie. That suitcase has our prints all over it, and so does Spooky."

"Fuck." Frankie seemed disgruntled. "I don't wanna wipe fingerprints off her fuckin' corpse with Wet-Naps."

"I don't give a fuck *what* you don't want. You got us into this mess, so you're gonna do the job. I ain't spendin' the rest of my life on Riker's with some guy named Luther usin' my asshole for a place to party. I can't believe how bad you fucked this up."

"It wasn't my fault, Nick." Frankie was pouting now. "She asked for it. She shouldn't oughta have said those things to me."

Nick pulled a Demerol tab from his pocket, showed it to his cohort. "You wipe down the bitch's body and then you can take your bang."

"Hey, thanks!"

The front of the Kwik-Mart shimmered in neon. There were only a few vehicles in the parking lot: a mint-condition '68 350 small-block Camaro that had been oddly spray-painted black, an old red pickup truck, and a gold Dodge Colt with a P.I.L. sticker in the back window. Nick and Frankie loped inside, Frankie beginning to sweat out some early withdrawal. "Shit, yeah!" Nick bellowed in the store. The man behind the counter, who wore a turban and bore a suspicious resemblance to the late Ayatollah Khomeini, jumped an inch off the floor at Nick's celebratory outburst. What was Nick celebrating? There was a little television behind the counter, the Yankees game on, and somebody named Giambi just hit a grand slam. The score was now 15 to 1.

And it was only the sixth inning.

"I *knew* that big boat anchor was good for somethin'!" Nick railed happily. Frankie shrugged, wishing for a mainline. They bought Wet-Naps and big coffees, and as they headed back toward the Caddy, Nick said, "You know, Frankie, I've got a really good vibe about tonight, even after all the shit that happened with Spooky." He shook his head hopefully. "When the Yankees beat the shit out of Baltimore, great things happen."

"Uh, yeah," Frankie replied, scratching himself. "I need to take a bang."

Nick dropped his coffee when he reached to open the car door. It splashed all over his shoes.

"Nick," Frankie asked. "What'choo drop your coffee for?"

Nick didn't answer. Instead his eyes rolled up into his head and he fainted, toppling to the pavement.

Frankie looked into the back seat and noted at once that the suitcase was gone.

"—two grand slams in the bottom of the ninth inning against the generally automatic Mariano Rivera," the tinny voice announced. "Yes, folks, it's a record-setting comeback as the Baltimore Orioles beat the New York Yankees, 16 to 15!"

Callused fingers, tinged in green light, snapped the old Philco radio off. Spooky wasn't dead, by the way. This might seem beyond belief, but in truth she hadn't actually broken her neck against the edge of the coffee table, nor had she suffered any manner of vertebral fracture or spinal-cord-transection. The impact had merely pinched her seventh and eighth cervical nerves, resulting in a reduced heart and respiratory rate and temporary neuromuscular paralysis. The tourniquets had prevented death from blood-loss. Hence, Spooky was alive.

And not in a very good mood when she regained consciousness.

Those motherfuckin' tube-steaks, she thought. *Goombah morons can't do any-fuckin'-thing right.*

She lay in the front footwell of a vehicle whose suspension springs creaked mercilessly over the back road's pot holes and dips. At first Spooky couldn't see—er, well, she could see enough to note that her legs had been summarily amputated, but that was about it. Above her, she made out faint green light, which she presumed were dashboard lights, but her vision was still too blurry to see the driver.

The driver, incidentally, was possessed of a very complex belief in providence. Twice a year he made these aimless drives all the way up the east coast and all the way back, not to visit relatives or to see sights, but simply to *be*. To contemplate himself. It proved a very self-actualizing experience. He'd merely pulled over at the Kwik-Mart, purchased a bag of Beechnut chewing tobacco, and had been walking back out of the store when—*poof!*—the inclination had struck him to look into the back of that big Cadillac. He'd seen the suitcase there and had simply taken it. It was providence, see?

Providence had told him to do that.

"Why, hey there," the driver said when he noticed the head on the torso moving. "How you feelin'?"

"What kind of a dick for-brains question is that, you old fuck?" the torso replied in the softest voice. "I've been armless for eleven motherfuckin' years and tonight the mafia-version of Laurel and Hardy cut my legs off in a motherfuckin' Howard Johnsons. How the fuck do you *think* I feel?"

"I understand your plight, hon, and there really ain't no cause fer profanation. Not now. See, I'se savin' you from yer travails. Gettin' diseases, smokin' the drugs, gettin' cornholed by fellas . . . it's the negertive forces'a the universe that's has caused you to veer from the blesséd path that yer supposed to take. I'se'll help you, missy—help you git'cherself back on the path."

"Huh?" Spooky said.

"Jus' you wait'n see, child," the driver said, his grizzled face eerie and green in the dash lights. He looked down at her through the darkness. "What'cher name, darlin'?"

"Spooky," Spooky said.

"Well, I'se pleased as punch ta meet'cha, Spooky." The driver smiled. "My name's Lud."

Grub Girl in the
Prison of Dead Women

Sure, hon, I got some time. I'll tell you the whole thing while you make up your mind. And this is no bullshit, either. You can read about it in the papers.

You know about Grubs, right? No? Shit, man, you from overseas or something? I'll make a long story short. "Grubs" are what they call us, same way they call black people niggers. Nice tag, huh? But I guess we *are* a little on the pasty side. But, look, don't get freaked out. I heard somewhere there are over ten thousand of us total. It all started with that ramjet thing, I don't know, a couple of years ago. Christ, I'm sure you heard about *that*. NASA and the Air Force were testing some new kinda plane, remotely piloted, they called it, flying it a hundred miles off the coast over the Atlantic. It was a nuclear ramjet or some shit, could fly indefinitely without fuel, no pilots, ran by computers. The idea was to have these things flying around all the time real high up. Cheap way to defend the nation. "The ultimate deterrent," the President said when they announced that they were gonna spend billions developing this flop. What they *didn't* announce was that plane kicked out a trail of some off-the-wall kinda radiation wherever it flew. The government wasn't worried about it 'cos it flew so high, the shit would go right out of the atmosphere. Well, something fucked up during one of the test flights, and one of these things wound up flying up and down the east coast at treetop level on something they called an "emergency urban alert bomb mode" for

41

something like five days before they could veer it off course over the sea and shoot it down. Thing was flying over *cities,* for shit's sake. And I was one of the ones lucky enough to get rained on by this thing.

I'd just come up from the docks down there, you know, by the Market Square, and I was walking up toward Clay Street. 'Rome, my pimp, he usually picked me and his other two girls up at about four a.m. Best time for us alley girls to turn tricks is after two, after the bars are closed 'cos then the cops stop buzzing the street to bust our chops. Fuckin' cops, nine times outa ten when they catch you, all they do is make you give 'em a blowjob, then let you go. Anyway, here I am, hoofing it up to Clay after turning about five tricks, and then there's this rumble way down deep in my belly and this sound like slow thunder, and I look up and see this ugly motherfuckin' thing flying about hundred feet over my head. Didn't know what to make of it. It looked like a big black kite in the sky, and when it passed, I could see this weird blue-green glow coming out of the back of the thing, its engines, I guess. I died a couple hours later, and the next day I woke up a grub.

There was a big whupdeedo for a little while. All of a sudden there were ten thousand dead people walking around and not knowing what the fuck hit them. President called an emergency meeting or some shit. Oh, you should've heard all the fancy talk they were spouting. At first they were gonna "euthanize" us "to safeguard the societal whole from potential contraindications," until some egghead at CDC verified that we weren't psychotic or contagious or radioactive or anything. Then some asshole Republican senator made a big pitch about how we should be "socially impounded." "Protean symtomologies," see, that's what they were worried about. These shitheads wanted to round us all up and put us on an island somewhere! It all blew over, though, after the activists started gearing up, and they let us be. After all, grubs are people too.

It didn't hurt really. Just felt sick for a few minutes, got a headache, puked, and died. Woke up the next day feeling pretty much the same as I always did. Woke up a Grub, and that's my story.

We call live people "pink" or "pinkies," and they call us Grubs. Only fair, they got names for us, we got names for them. 'Rome didn't get it, the prick, he stayed pink, and so did his other two hookers. The shit from the plane wouldn't get you if you were in a car or under a roof. About a dozen other hookers got it, though, 'cos they were out on the street just like me when that fucked up plane flew by, and now every pink hooker in the city hates us. See, johns want Grubs more than pink girls 'cos we're cheaper and we ain't got diseases. AIDS, herpes, and all that shit, I had it all when I was pink, but not no more, and a john knows that if he buys himself a nut with a grub he ain't gonna catch nothing.

Here's why I killed 'Rome, though. After I got grubbed, he got this brainstorm that he could really cop a bundle off me with the kinks. He'd work me right out of his crib, hitting johns up for a couple hundred bucks an hour! These sick fucks'd come in and do anything they wanted, and I mean *anything*. Bondage, S&M, scat, that sort of shit. 'Rome's only rule was that they weren't allowed to break any bones or cut off any parts. These kinks were a trip, let me tell you. You'd be surprised how many really sick motherfuckers there are in the world. They'd tie me up, jack me out, stick needles in my tits, shit in my mouth, you fuckin' name it.

Well, I started to get sick of this shit real fast. Here's this scumbag making cash hand over fist offa my ass, and I don't get shit out of it. So I . . .

Well, if you wanna know the details, I busted a toilet tank cover over his head one night, cut his belly open, and ate his guts.

Hell. Sometimes a girl's gotta do what she's gotta do.

See, grubs can only eat raw stuff. You eat regular food like the pinkies and the shit don't come out, you bloat up. There was this one gal named Sue who got grubbed just like me—blonde, kinda heavy set, *really* big tits—and she just goes on eating the regular shit that the pinkies eat, and one day I saw her walking past the hotel and, I swear, she's big as Jabba the Hut, and before she could make it to the bus stop, she, like, *exploded* right there in the street, made one holy hell of a mess. And this shithead Republican senator I was telling you about, you should've heard the guy, like because we can only eat raw stuff, that means we're gonna go on some zombie rampage eating people in the streets like some horror movie so that was his case for "socially impounding" us. Glad that asshole's shit didn't fly. Of course, it probably sounds pretty hypocritical of me, since I just got done telling you I chowed down on 'Rome insides. I just figured it was the thing to do, that's all. I got tired of being used by this scumbag, so I did the job on him. It wasn't like his guts tasted any better than anything else—grubs don't have a sense of taste.

One good thing about being a grub hooker, though, you start to stick up for yourself. You get a case of the ass and you don't take shit anymore. The rule had always been no girl works solo. You wanna work the street, you gotta have a pimp. Ask any hooker in any city in the world. You try to work solo, you get your face beat to mush or wind up in some dumpster with your throat cut. We'd always be too afraid to fight back, stand up for ourselves, you know? Shit, most girls are strung out anyway. I was. Back when I was pink, I was firing up scag four times a day, had to shoot up into my foot 'cos the veins on my arms all collapsed and turned black. I'd turn over my take to 'Rome every night like clockwork, and he'd keep me in junk, and that was all I cared about. When you're strung out, you really don't have a soul anymore. Yeah, turning my tricks, keeping 'Rome happy, and getting my fix—that's all there was for me. It was hell, let me tell you. But after I got grubbed, I didn't need the scag anymore, and it finally dawned on me that I didn't need 'Rome, either. All the other grubs working the street got the same gist, and all of a sudden a lot of pimps were winding up in body bags. The pink girls, sure, they're all still in their stables, but their pimps don't fuck with us grubs 'cos they know that if they do, they'll wind up just like 'Rome.

Fuck 'em.

And this fuckhead senator? He starts this shit about we'll destabilize the work base, how we gotta be segregated because employers will be hiring grubs instead of pinkies 'cos we can work round the clock, but then the congress passed a law against it. Of course, prostitution's still illegal but around here at least, the cops don't fuck with the grubs. It's a real laugh. We give 'em the creeps, so they just let us do our thing and leave us alone.

Er, I should say, they *used* to. But the new congress changed all that and fast. Now it's roundup time, hoss. If you're a Grub and you so much as spit on the sidewalk, there'll be some John Law motherfucker waiting to lock you up.

It was a plainclothes U.S. Marshal that busted me. Just my luck. "You're under arrest for sexual solicitation," he was nice enough to tell me only *after* he came in my mouth. "You motherless dickcheese ball-bag-stinking pig motherfucker!" I yelled back. I was gonna bust his coconut right there in the unmarked but before I could—*PAP!*— he hit me with a round from his track-operated spicule pistol, and that was it for me.

Regular weapons don't work on Grubs—we're dead, you know? So the pigs started making new kinds of guns that would paralyze us. Tubocurarine darts, electromagnetic-pulse nets, milliwave disrupters. When I came to, some fat DO—stands for Detention Officer—a guy named Stryker, he was finishing up a body-cavity search while I was chained to a wall. The fucker had his hand so far up my ass I thought he was trying to stick his fingers out my mouth.

"I want a fucking lawyer!" I screamed.

"Lawyer? Don't you watch the news? You're dead, bitch. Civil rights don't apply to dead people anymore. Thank God the Republicans are back in office. We can do anything we want to you grub scumbags."

45

When he finished fishing in my bowels, he jerked off on my ass, then let a half dozen more DOs gang-bang me right there against the wall. The last guy pissed up my ass, for posterity, I guess.

So that's it in a nutshell. The new administration dropped all the previous non-discrimination laws. Grubs weren't considered people anymore, so we were no longer entitled to humane treatment. That $10 blowjob got me a five-year sentence in this stone motel they call the Alderton Federal Rehabilitation Center. We'd heard rumors about this joint on the street; it was a Grubs-Only prison. Torture, slave labor, experiments. I learned the score here real quick; any Grubs that were good-looking got assigned to the Behavioral Segregation Wing. They called it the Fuck Farm. Gang rape was the order of the day, and so were kink jobs. In the old days, if the pinkies fucked with us we'd just pop their heads open and scarf their brains—Grubs are a lot stronger than pinks. But we couldn't fight back anymore because all inmates were fitted with UV nodes.

I remember the day I went in for my "fitting."

The sign on the door read: OBEDIENCE IS VIRTUE, but below that was another sign:

IMPLANTATION UNIT.

Stryker and some egghead tech had me strapped down to a padded table. The tech slit each of my nipples with a scalpel, stuck something about the size of a marble in each tit, then sewed me up. Then he slit open my clitoris and repeated the procedure. Sounds nasty but it was really no big deal: Grubs don't feel pain . . . er, at least that's what I'd always thought.

DO Stryker grinned down. "From now on, Grub, you do everything we say."

"Don't count on it, pig," I told him. "Oh, and by the way, your mother blows farm animals."

"What we've done, inmate," the tech informed me, "is surgically implant Bofors Model 250 ultraviolet-wave transponders into your most sensitive mammarian and genital nerve clusters. Upon activation, each transponder node will become energized with 20,000 nanounits of collective ultraviolet-band energy. In spite of the fact that you're clinically dead, this energy will flood the target dendron/axon ganglia, replenishing all electrical synaptic impulses—hence, causing pain that can only be described as incalculable."

"Drink my zombie piss," I replied.

"Mouthy little whore, ain't she?" Stryker chuckled, unstrapping me. I got up off the table, still groggy from the tubocurarine darts they'd been zapping me with. "But she'll soon learn that silence is golden."

"The only thing golden is the shower I'm gonna give you when I get out of this cement Ramada. Too bad your pappy didn't pull out early and leave his peckersnot on the floor. World'd be a better place."

"I'd take the officer's warning under serious advisement," the tech said. "The Bofors Model 250 is decidedly effective."

When you're a zombie, your life is bad enough. Grubs don't like to be intimidated.

And I guess I always did have a big mouth.

"How about I cut your cock off and fuck you in the ass with it?"

"You think this is a joke?" Stryker whipped out the sending unit, like a tv remote. "If I tell you to shit on the floor and eat it, you'll shit on the floor and eat it."

I dragged up a big chest oyster and hocked it in his face. "Eat that."

Ever heard of the Chicago Fire? That's what I felt like when the ever dutiful Detention Officer Stryker tapped my ID number into that sending unit. First my tits and pussy felt warm, tingling . . . then— *WHAM!* I felt alive again, all right, and that tech geek wasn't kidding about the pain. Like a brand-new Red Devil razor blade being slowly dragged through the middle of my clit, and a channel-lock on each nipple, a sewing needle in each eye, and a drill bit in my brain--that's what the pain all added up to when Stryker "activated" me.

"Gonna be a good girl now?" Stryker asked.

The ultraviolet waves surged through me. My spine arched back like a u-bolt, and I hit the floor. There was a sound somewhere that reminded me of squealing tires, but eventually I realized it was me—screaming.

"Here's your golden shower, bitch." I just lay there flopping like a fish on a hot plate. Stryker must've pulled a ten-beer piss on me, which upped the current transfer . . . and doubled the pain.

"Be a good girl now and do what I told you."

More needles, more channel-locks, more razors sliding . . . Just when it felt like my eyeballs would rupture, I . . . well.

I did it.

Shrieking like a baby in a furnace, I shit on the floor and ate it.

Stryker and his boys ran the Bev-Seg unit. Since Grubs don't sleep, they'd work us pretty much round the clock. First thing every morning they'd take us to the "Dining Hall." Brother, this was no Four Seasons. What they'd feed us was this goulash of what they called "rendered livestock." Mostly diseased pigs and chickens that wouldn't pass USDA, they'd get the shit from local farms and grind it up in hoppers. Um-um good.

After that, General Work Block. Cleaning up this federal outhouse, whatever needed to be done: swabbing toilets, mopping floors, cleaning the dumpsters and greasepits. Along the way me and the other girls'd sometimes catch glimpses of the other wings. Males Grubs, and any Grub girls who weren't good-looking, they'd be used for CDC research and Defense Corp experiments. But it was mainly curiosity when you get right down to it. The government still didn't know a whole lot about Grubs, so they'd do all these experiments to see what happened when you fucked with one. Starvation, for instance, wouldn't kill a Grub; you'd just get down to literally skin and bones. They had an entire wing full of Grubs who hadn't been allowed to eat for over a year. Then there were the transplants: putting live organs into dead people, usually animals guts and shit like that. There was a rumor that the R&D techs had successfully transplanted two heads onto a single Grub. Ordnance Development was worse: the military using Grubs to test new bullets, landmines, and rockets on. When things got too hot, they'd send us in for the cleanup— Jesus. It was mostly pieces we carried out of there. The Ectogenics Lab was reserved for Halfers—a Halfer is a Grub who'd only partly turned: half dead, half alive, and they'd fuck around with the ovaries on these Halfer chicks, knock them up, and see what came out.

You name it, these sick fucks did it, anything for a kick: microwaving, broiling, freezing. Brain transplants, lobotomies, transfusions. Whatever turned them on. It was enough to turn even a dead girl's stomach.

Next was RT—Rehabilitative Therapy. They'd make us sit in a room four hours a day and watch snuff films, live S&M, executions, car-wreck and ER footage. This was supposed to "cure" us, showing us what a life of crime would lead to. Gimme a fucking break! One time they showed this flick of a bunch of stoners with ten-inch herpetic cocks pulling a train on some junkie chick eight-months' pregnant. They fucked her so hard she breaks her water and miscarries right there on the floor. So I look in the back of the room and half the DOs are so boned up watching this flick they're jerking off! If anybody in the slam needed rehab, it was them, not us.

After that was another Work Block, then a trip to the Hygiene Unit; the DOs'd watch while we soaped each other down, then they'd hose us off and get us ready for LockDown. See, they'd want us squeaky clean before the fun began. They might as well've put a revolving door on our cells with all the men coming in and out. First shift was for VIPs: bigwheels in the state government, Prison Admin chiefs, staffers, Public Safety officials, the Warden and his suits. One hard tubesteak after another. Then the guards themselves would get their turn, and that was worse. These guys were real kinks and psych-jobs, especially Stryker. Ass-fuck parties, fletch parties, scat, gang-bang face-fucks. One girl threatened to bite the next cock someone tried to stick in her mouth, so they activated her UV implants and left them on all night. Then they took us to the Med Unit the next day and pulled all our teeth just to be safe.

Stryker particularly had it in for me: ordering other girls to shit on me, piss in my mouth, fist-fuck me. His favorite move was to buttfuck another chick and make me suck his jizz out of her ass. And what could I do about it? Jack shit. Any time I pitched a fit, he'd whip out his sending unit and activate my UV nodes. You learn fast in this place . . .

But don't worry. No way in holymotherfucking hell was I gonna take this shit for my whole hitch.

See, I had a plan.

A three-part plan. I had to do it just right, and it took months to get ready. Busting out of this shithole wasn't good enough. I had to get the rest of the Grubs out too, not to mention a few scores to settle.

Once a week it was my job to empty the trash in the Booking Unit. There were a lot of used tubocurarine darts in bottom of the can. Any chance I got I'd pinch a few, hid 'em in my cell later. Why? Because there was still a little curare left in cartridges . . .

Next was the geek in the Implantation Lab—and when I say geek I mean GEEK. This wuss made Mr. Rogers look tough, and it was a good bet he'd never been laid. Next time I got mop duty in the IL, I put the make on him hard. I mean, I ain't bragging but ya gotta admit—am I good-looking or what? Once I stepped out of my cellblock overalls, I had this guy worshipping me, wound up fucking his brains out. Wore his virgin pecker out, I did.

And when the asshole wasn't looking, I pinched one of his scalpels . . .

Part Three was the toughest part. See, in 2003 the NRC authorized liquid-plasma isotope reactors for industrial use, and they had one of these little Three Mile Islands providing all the power for the prison.

If I could get a key to the Fuel Core Station . . .

At night, when the gang bangs and kink parties were over, I'd just sit in my cell and dream. Even dead people dream. I'd think back to the way things were when I was working the street. Didn't ask for much, and I never ripped off a john in his life who didn't have it coming. Sure, I killed some pimps and baddies, but they had it coming too. All I ever wanted was to do my thing, mind my own business, and live my life. But the Feds and the pigs and the U.S. Marshals came along with their Dr. Strangelove Big Brother bullshit. What I ever do to them? And—what?—it's my fault their fuckin' nuke-powered plane crashed and turned 10,000 people into Grubs? Fuck that.

And fuck them.

I knew I had to make my move just before LockDown. I wanted as many government bigwheels in here as possible. But I knew I had to get Stryker alone.

So when they were taking us to chow before LD, I hocked a lunger right into Stryker's face and said, "Your mother sucks cocks in hell."

Stryker grinned. He was glad I did it. "You're a ballsy little whore, ain't ya? Like to run that cocksuck zombie-whore mouth of yours."

"Your daddy must've had shit on his dick when he knocked your mama up with you."

His grin turned demonic. "Baby, I'll cut your head off and jerk off in your mouth."

I cracked out a laugh. "Man, all you can *do* is jerk off. Can't lay any *serious* dick on a woman to save your life."

"Think so?"

"Gimme a break? A peter-licking, panty-wearing, no-hard-on

little candy-ass like you?"

"Yeah, maybe I'll activate you till your tits pop and your hair burns off. See how the smart-mouth Grub Girl likes *that* action."

"Talk is cheap. You can light me up with that pissant UV thing all you want. I *like* pain, pig. Gets me horny, you know, for a *real* man? Too bad there ain't any in this armpit. I'll bet you ten bucks your dick wouldn't last a minute in my pussy."

He stared me down, nodding. "You're on, bitch. I'm gonna fuck you so hard your brains'll be squirting out your ears, and when I'm done I'm gonna throw your whore ass into Isolation and leave your transponders on for a month."

"I hear ya talking, Liberace."

"Get the rest of these dead bitches to chow," Stryker barked to his sergeants. "I'll be taking this one here back to her cell for a private consultation."

He dragged me by the hair to my cell, and then I knew I had him.

By then, see, I'd collected enough curare from the used cartridges to fill an entire dart. Stryker didn't even have time to get his pants down before I had that baby stuck right in his fat red neck.

"What . . . what did you . . . do?"

He came to about an hour later, and an hour was plenty of time to do the job. I held up the scalpel I jacked from that nerd tech. "See this, asshole? I cut the UV implants out of myself."

Eventually his crossed eyes began to focus, incomprehension on his face.

"Whaaaa . . ."

"Then I sewed them back up in your nutsack."

Now the incomprehension turned to slow horror. He reached down to his ballbag, felt around, and then moaned. You could hear the little nodes clicking in there. "God in heaven . . . please don't—"

"Guess we better test 'em huh?"

"Noooooo! Pleeeeeease!"

I tapped my own ID into the sending unit and lit DO Stryker up like the fucking Fourth of July. Yes sir-ee. 60,000 nanounits of ultraviolet-band energy right smack-dab into his family jewels.

The fat fuck screamed louder than a truck horn, and I gotta tell ya, it was fun watching him flop around on the floor like a tadpole out of water. I had a mind to just leave him there like that, but . . .

There was still work to do.

"Punch in the passcode," I ordered.

I'd marched him down to the Utility Wing. Shiftchange was over so the halls were clear.

"No way," he said. "I can't. It's a security breach. The core's running—"

"Punch in the passcode and open the door, motherfucker, unless you want me to cook your nuts again. By the time I'm done, they'll look like a couple of fried chicken gizzards."

He was crying now, blubbering like a baby. I showed him the sending unit, and that was all it took. He plipped in the code and the vault door sucked open.

WARNING, one sign read. NUCLEAR FUEL CORE IS *ON.* FATAL RADIOACTIVE DOSE AFTER TWENTY MINUTES.

Fatal? Sure. But not to somebody who's already dead.

I threw Stryker aside and jacked the fuel rods right out of the core chassis. The evac alarms went off immediately. "Don't leave me in here!" Stryker bellowed. "I'll die!"

"Buddy," I said, "five minutes from now you'll be *praying* to die." Then I activated him again. It was tempting not to stay there and watch awhile—no, the meltdown wouldn't hurt *me*, but I had the other Grubs to get out. I took one last gander at Stryker: screaming, shitting and pissing himself, blood leaking out his eyes, ears, and mouth, his hair baking off and his crotch smoking. Man, it was sweet.

Then I left and closed the door.

The reactor cooked-off about a half-hour later; the radiation took out every pinkie in the joint before they could reach safe distance. As for the rest of the Grubs, I used Stryker's block keys to open their cells and we all waltzed out of that shitpit like we owned the place. Out front I could see the Warden and a bunch twerps from the Governor's Office crawling across the asphalt with their skin running off their bodies. So long, chumps.

So that's the story, pal. Don't believe me? Read about it in the papers. Oh, and that plainclothes U.S. Marshal who busted me in the first place? You probably read about him in the papers too. I spotted the motherfucker the first week I was back working the street. Yanked his cock and balls off then pulled his intestines out his ass. The fucker looked like he had a *tail* when I was done! I mean, come on, he had it coming. I never fucked with no one who didn't fuck with me first.

But how about you, pal? Made up your mind yet? You're kind of cute, if you don't mind me saying so, and—holy Christ—is that Godzilla in your pants or are you just happy to see me? Ten bucks, partner, best blowjob of your life, and if I'm lying, I'll give you your money back.

So what do you say?

Good man!

The Dritiphilist

"I have this . . . problem," he admitted.

"Believe me, everyone who's ever sat in that chair has a problem," related Dr. Marsha Untermann. "Not a typical problem but a grievous one. A problem so incalculable—and so *aberrant*—that it rocks the imagination." The woman's gaze thinned. A long elegant finger traced a graceful chin. "You're here for a reason—your own rehabilitation. You're scared. You're scared that I might find your 'problem' so deviant or absolutely appalling that I will insist that you leave my office at once and never come back."

Nougat-brown eyes leveled at him.

"Yes," he croaked. "I'm . . . very afraid of that."

"Because if that happens, you'll have nowhere to go?"

"Yes," he said.

"You probably think that there is no one else in the world like you. That's why you've refrained from seeking help in the past, correct?"

"Yes."

Dr. Untermann leaned back in the chair behind her desk. She smiled as thinly as her gaze. "Then your fears are without foundation. I do not turn patients away, however foul their problems—or their crimes—may seem. It's my job. I do my job. And I think I can safely say that this 'problem' of yours?" She lit a long cigarette and shook her head. "I've heard *much* worse."

The smoke spewed from her lips like a ghostly fluid. Her eyes opened wider, inquisitive, coldly promising.

"Tell me about this problem of yours," she said.

Barrows' suit cost more than the average resident of Seattle earned in a month. As an investment banker for Jenkins, Harris, & Luce, he could afford it. He could afford the Aston Martin Zagato with the turbo'd 5.3-liter V8, he could afford the Movado gold watch, and he could afford the waterfront penthouse suite on Alaskan Avenue.

One thing he could not afford, however, was to allow anyone of import to see him—

Well . . .

Better to put it this way. If Barrows made $500,000 in one year—*that* was a bum year. Investment banking involved a certain alchemy of which Barrows possessed the cabalistic necromancer's wand. Objectively, his profession entailed moving clients' money from one bank to another, which sounded simple. In truth, though, knowing where and when to move the money, and for how long, was what made his clients and himself preposterously wealthy. In other words, William Barrows had a reputation to maintain, a reputation upon which his financial solvency depended.

Already out of place in the Armani suit, he walked slowly down the sidewalk past the county courthouse on Third Avenue, right alongside the bums and drug addicts wandering in their plight to a stinking nowhere. Yet Barrows scarcely saw them. He walked steadily onward, his eyes roving the sidewalk's cement for . . .

His heart jumped when he heard the sound . . .

The sound of a man clearing his throat and expectorating loudly.

The ever-familiar *splat* on the sidewalk came next, and next after that came Barrows' nearly full erection. Up ahead, he saw it. A derelict in filthy beard and rotten clothes had coughed up a wad of phlegm from his homeless-roughened lungs, and spat it on the sidewalk.

Oh, God, Barrows thought just as a normal man would think upon entering the bedroom of a beautiful woman for the first time, or watching that risky bond fund skyrocket and split.

Barrows caught the glint: a lumpen gem. It lay there waiting for him, freshly green, savory and mystical. Barrows' Guccis clicked up and stopped, and now he was standing there, feet apart, over the treasure.

He was discreetly protecting it from haphazard trample.

For someone to walk on it would be vandalism. It would be yanking the needle from an addict's vein and cruelly emptying the syringe out the window. Barrows was *guarding* it, in other words, while at the same time trying to appear normal.

He glanced at his watch, frowned like a Straussberg method actor waiting for a bus; he was Hitchcock in a phone booth. He had to be careful. He could not allow himself to be seen doing what he was about to do.

He waited, calmly tapping his foot. Eventually the pedestrian traffic broke: no one coming down the block from either side.

Oh, God . . .

Like magic, then, Barrows produced the two index cards from his suit pockets. He knelt very quickly, scooped up the lump of phlegm in the cards, then turned and walked briskly back up the sidewalk.

He ducked behind one of the courthouse's high brick pillars. No one was there.

Thank you, God . . .

Then he licked the hock of phlegm off the card, sucked it around in his mouth like a delectable raw oyster, and swallowed it whole.

He closed his eyes, stood as if paralyzed. He felt the still-warm phlegm sink to his gut, and then he signed in bliss, similar to the bliss felt by a crack addict after the first hit of the day off the pipe.

This was Barrows' rush–not cocaine, not heroin, not sex nor drink nor gambling.

It was phlegm.

Hence was his plight, the macabre curse which had held him captive for most of his adult life. Barrows was a phlegm-eater.

He couldn't help it, and he never knew why.

This is so wrong, he thought every time he scraped up a lump and ate it. What seemed even more wrong was what followed after he swallowed: a titan sexual surge. Most times he was able to contain himself until he got home, other times no. Other times he'd slink into a urine-fetid alley or between a high bank of bushes, to vigorously masturbate.

Seeing phlegm on the street lit a oracular fire in him. It nearly stripped him of all sanity, of everything that could be called healthy.

Barrows had to have it.

He had to eat it.

Picture a person stumbling across the desert. This person has not drunk water in days. Suddenly that person, close to death, happens upon a clear cold babbling brook . . .

To Barrows, the babbling brook was sputum. The dirtier the better. The more catastrophically disgusting, the more he'd need it. Homeless bums were best, the people literally rotting in the alleys, hacking up clumps of respiratory discharge from soiled and emphysematic lungs. Virtual *wads* of congestion. Sometimes the chunks were coppery with blood, or uniquely textured by bits of cancerous lung tissue. Sometimes the clumps contained mysterious grit.

All the better for Barrows.

He had to have it. He had to scrape it raw off the sidewalk and eat it, hoping no one would bear witness. He could imagine the reaction of an associate partner walking down the street one day and seeing Barrows scarfing bum phlegm. He could imagine what the firm's president might say upon hearing of this. With every day that went by, and with every chunk of some rummie's hock that he ate, Barrows knew he was existing on borrowed time.

Once a Seattle cop had seen him, and though Barrows could not conceive that eating phlegm off the sidewalk violated the law, he was grateful that the constable had received a call on his radio at the same time. Barrows did not want to have to explain what he was doing. A number of homeless had seen him too, but he needn't explain to them.

Sometimes he paid the dregs of the local prostitutes to cough into his mouth. Sometimes he'd walk right up to paralyzed bums rotting in alleyways and pay them $100 to drag up a giant loogie and hack it up into his hand, after which he'd eat it like a culinaire savoring Nicouli ossetra caviar off of toast points. Once he'd paid an obese homeless woman on Jackson Street to cough up a big one into his mouth. She'd smelled worse than anything Barrows' olfactory senses had ever experienced, but she'd obliged and then some, hacking up a blob of phlegm the size of a baby's fist. When Barrows had rolled it around on his tongue, he'd found a rotten tooth, which he'd swallowed with the rest of the prize.

Bums and whores and Seattle's constant human street detritus were one thing, but he knew he had to be careful, more careful than he'd been in the past. He couldn't have people on the street recognizing him, oh no, not with his picture constantly in the state market news, not with his picture in *Forbes* and the financial trade magazines. But too often it seemed that the longer this grotesque curse went on, the more he became lost in it.

With every glob he slurped down, he realized how wrong it was, how demented and abnormal. And for the two decades that had transpired since his first indulgence at age twenty, he'd always assumed that his sickness was so remote, and so insulated, as to be totally exclusive to himself.

What could he say to his doctor? What could he say to a shrink? *I have this problem, see? I have to eat phlegm.*

No, no. He could not say that, because he couldn't believe that anyone else on the surface of the earth could be stricken with such a bizarre and filthy addiction.

Barrows, in his curse, felt alone in the world. Until—

He'd been hunting for a fresh wad, after work as usual, stalking the most rank warrens of Third and Yesler—the "Bum" district. *Damn it!* came the desperate thought. He itched, junkie-like, when he saw the *droves* of people milling up and down. The Kingdome loomed, reminded him that baseball season was in full swing; the extra pedestrians would make his travail all the more difficult.

Wait, he thought.

No other choice.

Barrows ducked under the pillared cover of the King County Courthouse, amongst a coterie of employees out for a smoke break.

He stood there for hours.

Waiting.

By eight p.m., he was cross-eyed in his need. His fingernails had dug crescent gouges into the meat of his palms, and his face felt was slicked with sweat. He watched the whores flit by across the street, each of whom would be grateful to hack into his mouth for a C-Note; he watched the bums straggle, spitting their precious wares onto the sidewalk.

Too far away for Barrows to claim.

The sun sunk. He came close to chewing a hole in his lower lip as he waited. Then—

An obese, bearded man in a wheelchair (wearing a plaid dress, of all things [but this was Seattle]) rolled by and hacked loudly. A wad of blackish phlegm landed only feet before the place where Barrows stood.

Barrows' heart picked up.

He ducked out, an index card in each hand. Anxious glances up and down the street showed him meager pedestrian traffic.

He scooped up the wad, walked to the big brown garbage can behind the bus stop, then knelt as if to tie his shoe.

He didn't tie his shoe.

His lips pulled the fresh lump off the card. He sighed as his tongue squashed the briny lump between his tongue and the roof of his mouth. He savored and swallowed.

Jesus . . .

It was all he could do, then, not to stick his hand right down into his pin-striped Italian slacks and beat himself off. His knees wobbled at the rush. He was *fixing* as the lump went down.

Jesus God . . .

When the rush lifted, and his vision cleared, he heard a scuff to his left. *The bus shelter,* he thought but hardly cared. Suddenly, though, the sidewalk was vacant, and in the bus shelter, he saw—

A tall, haggard man, another "bum." Jeans smudged black with dirt, long hair, beard flecked with bits of food and boogers. The back of his dun-colored jacket read KING STREET GOSPEL HOMELESS SHELTER, and he was doing the most unusual thing:

He was—

What the . . .

With a piece of cardboard, he was scraping up a pile of vomit in the bus shelter; in fact, he was scraping it up rather meticulously.

The vomit looked like chunky pink oatmeal.

Then he flapped the granular puke into a plastic Zip-Loc bag. He craned his long neck, caught Barrows staring at him.

A snarl like an animal, then the ran man away, carrying his plastic bag full of bum vomit with him.

"That's when I knew it," Barrows admitted to Dr. Untermann. "When I saw that guy—that bum—scraping up the vomit off the sidewalk and carrying it away . . ." He closed his eyes, rubbed his temples. "That's when I knew—"

"That you weren't the only one with a severe and incomprehensible problem," Marsha Untermann finished for him. "Hmm. Collecting vomit."

61

"Yes. Collecting it, putting it in a bag." Barrows looked up at the comely psychiatrist. "I don't even want to think what he does with it later."

"He probably eats it," Dr. Untermann bluntly offered. "It's a form of dritiphily."

Barrows' lower lip hung down in bewilderment. "A form of—"

"Dritiphily, or dritiphilia. It's part of the clinical scope of what we now think of as an OCD—an obsessive-compulsive disorder." Her manicured index finger raised. "But it's very rare, to the extent that it's scarcely acknowledged anymore." Her finely lined eyes blinked once, then twice. "I'm not quite sure why."

But Barrows still sat in confusion, facing this elegant, refined woman behind the broad cherrywood desk. *What did she say?* he thought. "Drit—"

"Dritiphily," her lightly colored lips reiterated.

"There's a name for it? There's a . . . diagnosis?"

"Yes, er—there *was.* It disappeared from the diagnostic indexes in the late-sixties. For thirty years there was a listing in the DSM. That's the shrink's battle book, the *Diagnostic and Statistical Manual of Mental Disorders.* But Dritiphily, as a diagnosis, vanished once the later editions were released. Instead, it's been sub-categorized into some of the newer disorders."

Barrows felt rocked. "You mean there's actually . . . a name . . . for my . . . problem?"

"Yes," she quickly replied. "And you're rather lucky in that my main office is located in Seattle. Besides myself, there are only two other psychiatrists on the west coast who deal in such afflictions. One's in L.A., the other in San Diego."

Barrows paused to look at her—this gracile and unique specialist who had agreed to see him at a rate of $450 per hour. The fee, to Barrows, was pocket change to a typical man. He'd pay anything— *anything*—for help.

Dr. Marsha Untermann was probably over fifty, sharply

attired, graceful in manner, her face calm yet her myrtle-green eyes intense. The straight, shining dark gray hair—cut just above the shoulders—gave her an exotic cast, not an aged one; she was high-bosomed, strikingly attractive. Barrows thought of a Lauren Hutton or a Jacqueline Bissett. He'd found her simply by searching the Department of Mental Hygiene's website; Dr. Untermann's office address and number had been the only listing under the CRITICAL OUT-PATIENT/ABNORMAL PSYCHIATRY heading.

To Barrows, "abnormal" was putting it mildly.

"So it was this derelict, this vagabond, that impelled you to contact me," she said more than asked.

"That's right." Barrows still felt tightly uncomfortable by all he'd confessed to. Nevertheless, something about her allayed him, like confessing to a nameless priest behind a screen. And he remembered what she'd told him earlier: *I've heard much worse.* Comforting words to Barrows but still . . .

How much worse? he wondered. It proved a terrifying question.

"I suspect, by your appearance, that you're a man of means?"

"I'm rich," Barrows said with no enthusiasm. "I'm an investment banker."

"Then you might appreciate this quite a bit. This derelict you saw, this precursor, this piece of human flotsam you saw whisking up vomit from the bus stop . . . you and he are essentially the same."

Barrows calculated this.

"You're rich, he's homeless and poor. You have the best of everything, he has nothing. Yin meets Yang, the capitalist meets the *victim* of capitalism. The man plugged *in* meets the man cast *out.* The two of you couldn't be more different from a societal standpoint." Her lips pursed momentarily. Then she added, "But sickness, Mr. Barrows, is relative."

Barrows found the point of little use—his selfishness, perhaps. His obliviousness in wealth. "I don't want to sound callus," he said, "but I didn't make this appointment to have you make me feel guilty about being rich."

"You *shouldn't* feel guilty," she replied. "You should feel accomplished. You should feel proud. You've done what most can't do."

Barrows found no use in this either, and he was not a man to beat around the proverbial bush. His voice roughened. "I usually make a million dollars a year but I have to eat *phlegm* off the street. That sounds crazy, but I'm *not* crazy. I need help. You're the expert. Don't patronize me. Help me."

Her bosom rose as she leaned back in her plush chair. "You're a dritiphilist, with erotomanic undertones. You eat phlegm and masturbate after doing so—that's not quite the same as someone who's an asthmatic or even a schizophrenic. There's no magic pill for dritiphily."

"Long-term psycho-therapy?" he frowned. "Is that it?"

"Possibly. But don't scoff so quickly at behaviorilist science. Freud was quite right in many of his tenets. Most psychological anomalies have a sexual base. And Sartre was right too. Existence proceeds essence. It is our *existence*, Mr. Barrows, which makes us what we are. Conversely, the inexplicable trimmings of that existence are what cause our mental problems."

Barrows sighed in frustration.

As the sun set in her Pioneer Square window, the shiny dark-gray hair seemed to glow from behind, like an angel's aura. *But this is one cold bitch of an angel,* he thought.

"Let me guess," Dr. Untermann posed. "You had a normal childhood."

"Yes."

"You were raised by loving and well-to-do parents."

"Yes."

"And you received an excellent education."

"Private school and Harvard Yard."

The woman didn't seem the least bit impressed. "And this

affliction of yours—it started in your late-teens?"

"I was twenty . . ."

"And your first sexual–or I should say *copulative*–experience came shortly before that?"

"Nineteen . . ." Barrows' eyes narrowed. She was hitting each nail directly on the head, which made him feel better. "You know a lot."

"Obsessive-compulsive disorders have many objective lay-lines." She seemed casual suddenly, even bored. "They're all different but they're all the same in certain ways. You probably married shortly after college?"

"Immediately after."

"But you didn't love her, did you?"

Barrows stalled. At first he was offended that she make such an accusation, but then he remembered that it was true.

"No," she went on. "You married her because you thought that wedlock—a *normal* incident—might guide you back to normalcy yourself."

Irritated, he shirked in his seat. "Yes."

Dr. Untermann lit another long, thin cigarette. A blur of creamy smoke appeared between her lips, then vanished in a blink. "Tell me about the circumstances of your divorce."

Barrows challenged her. "I'm not divorced," he said. "I'm still happily married."

"Mr. Barrows," she immediately sighed, "if you want to pay me $450 per hour to lie, then go right ahead. I'll take your money. But that's hardly productive now, is it?"

His smirk made his face feel hot. He felt like a naughty child. *This ice-queen is a real piece of work.* "Guess not," he admitted.

"Your marriage did *not* return you to normalcy, did it?"

"No."

"Your 'affliction' only increased, and you hid it from your wife until—"

Barrows loosened his collar. "Yes, until she caught me red-handed. She got the flu one week. She . . ."

"Go on. I'm your psychiatrist, Mr. Barrows. The more you tell me, the more I can help."

Barrows' shoulders slumped. "She caught me eating her Kleenex out of the wastebasket. In truth—"

"Yes?"

"—whenever she had a cold or the flu . . . I loved it." He rubbed his face in his hands. "All that Kleenex. All that snot and phlegm." It was like a treat, like a midnight snack.

When Barrows looked back up at Untermann, it was shamefully, between his fingers. But the curt, elegant face remained unchanged. It remained inquisitive, calculating. Not shocked.

He sat back up straight in the leather chair. "How come you're not disgusted?"

"For the same reason an oro-facial surgeon is not 'disgusted' by a critical burn victim. The same reason a dentist isn't disgusted by an abscess. Your job is ministering to the intricacies of finance, Mr. Barrows. My job treating bizarre and often repellent mental disorders. To me, however, they're not bizarre nor repellent. They're merely disorders."

Barrows was amazed at her professional detachment . . . so then he sought to challenge her again, not with lies this time, but with a simple question with which to gauge her response.

"Let me ask *you* something. May I?"

Coils of faint smoke drifted upward. "Yes, but I'll only answer if I deem it to be productive toward your therapy."

All right. By now Barrows couldn't deny a flirting attraction to her, and this seemed a sorry notion indeed. *I've just told this woman that I eat phlegm, that I pay bums to spit in my mouth. I'm sure she's just dying to go to the opera with me . . .*

"Earlier," he faltered to begin, "you said . . . that you've heard worse . . ."

"Oh, my God yes," she casually replied. "Mr. Barrows, you've come in here thinking that you're an unspeakable person because of your dritiphily, but believe me, that's nothing compared to some of the patients I've treated."

"*Really?*" he said, incredulous.

Dr. Untermann reeled off her list as casually as if reciting scores at a miniature golf match. "I've treated zoophiles and scatophiles and pedophiles. I've treated Munchausen Syndrome where women really do love their kids but can't help bringing them to near-death. I've treated women with Helsinki Syndrome, who fell in love with the men who tortured them in ways that beggar description. I had a strange 'pica' case where a teenage girl unconsciously collected dog stool—she'd carefully dry the stools and consume them—and I had a sexual-septicist once—a man obsessed with masturbating with a handful of his own feces. When I was at Georgetown, one of our case studies was an accountant who would collect used condoms from the alleys in Washington, D.C.'s red light district and eat them; he was operated on over a dozen times because the condoms would inflate with his own waste and cause massive and potentially fatal intestinal blockages. We had another man addicted to eating 'toe-cheese,' and yet another man—a Virginia rancher—who could only attain erection by sucking the drool off the lips of cattle." She exhaled more smoke, unperturbed. "Then we have what we call the 'packers.'"

"Puh-packers?" Barrows dared.

"Men and women who, behind closed doors, are habituated to filling their rectal and reproductive cavities with—well, with just about anything you can imagine. Hamsters, fish, billiard balls, live snakes, live bullfrogs, wines bottles, garden slugs. You name it. One man from Annandale, Virginia, would blow mealworms into his urethra through a plastic tube. A fourteen-year-old girl from—she was a military dependent from Walter Reed—would insert the tip of a turkey baster into her own urethra in order to repeatedly aspirate air into her bladder. Some people simply like to be *filled*, Mr. Barrows, for reasons that can never be clinically perceived. Then we've got the more common aberrations—the collectors: the gym teachers who collect dirty socks, the custodians who collect used tampons, the fetishists who break into houses and collect undergarments soiled by the so-called 'skidmarks.' Pedicurists who keep their clients' toenail clippings. Doctors who collect pus-drenched bandages, and nurses who collect enema nozzles to secret away back to their homes, to sniff and lick."

Barrows felt exhausted listening to this, and disgusted. But there was more . . .

"One of my colleagues at the Clifton T. Perkins Evaluation Center wrote an entire diagnostic paper on a dermatologist who would topically anesthetize appropriate prison patients and, with pliers, squeeze the 'milk' out of large moles, and lick it up. During my internship at the psych wing of the Fallaway Med Center, there was a nun who constantly volunteered for duty in places like Calcutta, Karachi, and the Sudan. Her sister superiors alerted us to her problem: she was cleaning the ears of the dying with Q-Tips and sucking off the wax."

Fuck, Barrows thought.

"Stercoraceous syndromes are actually even *more* common," she continued. "People obsessed with human excrement—their own or that of others. Adolf Hitler was said to be a stercoramanic; he liked to defecate on women's faces—poor Eva Braun, hmm? A reverse syndrome involves the opposite, clearly Freudian: people who can only become sexually aroused while being defecated *on.* The actual shit-*eaters* are called coprophiliacs or cacophiles—hence the children's colloquialism *caca.* You'd be surprised how many feces-eaters there are in the realms of modern mental disorder."

Barrows' head began to feel light from shock.

"We've even had a few vomit-eaters," the elegant woman added went on, "like the derelict you saw at the bus stop. People who can find no sense of actualization without the self-abasement of consuming the puke of strangers—they're called 'refluxomanics,' by the way. And though I've never actually met a phlegm-eater before, I've read several case files regarding them. So you needn't feel exclusive, Mr. Barrows. There are, indeed, other people sitting in the same boat as yourself."

Barrows needed a drink. Bad. *Phlegm-eater,* he thought. There it was, a single, simple term. "But you also called it . . . what?"

"Dritiphily—from the Middle English noun *drit,* meaning something akin to *human filth.* You see how obscure the base word is? It doesn't even actively exist in our language any more. But obsessive-compulsive symptomologies do indeed exist within a broad range of clinical verges. Utterly minor to the utterly *outré.* Your regrettable affliction—your dritiphily—is the most extreme manifestation of the poor soul who must count to ten every time they see a red truck, or must step on every third crack in the sidewalk."

Even Barrows, in his overall shock, had to take exception. "Paying rummies and sick street whores to spit in my mouth isn't exactly stepping on sidewalk cracks."

"Outwardly, no. But inwardly, it's all rooted in the same inception," the staid woman replied. "We simply have to *identify* that inception—in your particular case, Mr. Barrows—and then we'll disclose the proper avenue of your—"

"My cure?" Barrows said hopefully.

"Yes."

She turned her hand, raised her rice-paper wrist to cast a glance at her watch. "We still have plenty of time. I think we should go on."

"All right," Barrows agreed. "Please."

"So what have we done thus far? We've identified the more intricate manifestations of your dritiphily. We've established, through your own self-revelation, that you are habituated to eating phlegm, and that this ingestion is the only thing that permits you to achieve sexual arousal. Yes?"

Barrows didn't like the sound of that, but he kept reminding himself what he was here for. Hence, his reply: "Yes."

"Normal childhood, normal upbringing," she said more to herself. "Not at all uncommon. The *bad* childhoods, the *ab*normal upbringings—those are the environmental breeding grounds for the Henry Lee Lucases, the John Wayne Gacys, the Jeffrey Dahmers. But you're a successful investment financier, not a psychopath, not a serial-killer."

Thanks, Barrows thought.

"Instead, *your* anomaly is rooted *in between* those notions. It's hidden. It's secreted away somewhere. Think of a well-crafted clock, but with the tooth of one solitary gear broken. We will find that cog, Mr. Barrows, and we will fix it."

"You make it sound easy," his voice grated.

"It may be. How badly to do want to be cured?"

He looked up quickly. "I'll do anything. Pay . . . *anything.*"

"You're accustomed to throwing money at your problems," she acknowledged. "But that may not suffice here. Your mind is not a carburetor simply in need of a new gasket. But as your current psychiatrist, I'd be negligent in not informing you of some potential 'quick fixes.' There are, for instance, some rather radical treatments not endorsed by the APA, available in South America. Cariothiazine infusions which alter the chemistry of your brain, acupuncture, various aroma and thermal-therapies. Narco-synthesis and bio-feedback cycles. I'll admit, sometimes they work, but I can't recommend them."

Barrows sat closer to the edge of his seat, wringing his hands. "I'll try anything, and . . . I'll pay. I'll pay *a lot.*"

"So you've said. One thing I can recommend a bit more than the latter would be an aversion-therapy clinic in Köping, Sweden. Believe me, they'll cure you of anything—the hard way."

"I'll do it!" Barrows nearly shouted at her.

"I don't suppose that the $30,000-per-month in-patient fee would bother you. But I'll be honest in informing you that all too often these rather Pavlovian aversion techniques only eradicate one disorder to expeditiously replace it with another."

"Great. I go from eating phlegm to eating shit? No thanks," Barrows gruffed. He sat back, hands held out uselessly. "What then?"

"Your best chance for a successful recovery?"

"Tell me!"

Her long fingers idly rolled the cigarette, then crushed it out. "Your best chance for a successful recovery stands with what you've previously frowned at. Maintained—and expensive— psychotherapy," she said. "Certainly, I'm aware now that you're a man of considerable income, and, especially due to the nature of your profession, you may think that I'm merely recommending the option that would most benefit my own financial interest. Therefore, to reduce any such trepidations, I'd be happy to give you a list of other psychiatrists who would be happy to render a second opinion."

To hell with it, Barrows thought. Her staunch demeanor and cool locution told him enough: *She's it. Where else can I go? Fuckin' Sweden? Goddamn South America?* Besides, at the very least, she was attractive; Barrows, in fact, caught a quick fantasy in his mind: Sucking down a big green loogie and fucking her right there on the desk. Maybe if he put a gun to her head, she'd spit in his mouth. "That won't be necessary. I want you to treat me. Please."

"Fine," she said crisply and leaned forward. She began writing on a small tablet. "For the first month, our sessions will be five days a week, seven if necessary. You've told me that you typically embark upon your . . . need . . . when you leave work, correct?"

"Yes."

"So I'll schedule you for, say, six p.m? Will that suffice?"

"Yes," Barrows agreed.

"Instead of stalking down James Street every day after work, you'll be coming here." She finished writing, handed him a small slip of paper. "Here's a prescription for a drug called Hydroxyzine. Ten milligrams four times a day. It will help ease the physical aspects of your dependency. In the meantime, I'll schedule you at Harborview for a physical: blood tests, histamine counts, and the like, and also your first atropine injection, which helps take the edge off too. Then we'll set you up for a written battery—MMPIs, TATs and TEDs, the Baley Scales and the Rorschachs—these are tests which might seem frivolous to you, but their conclusions will help me get a better fix on the more systematized aspects of your psychological make-up."

"I'll do it," Barrows said without pause.

"Try to cessate your urges. You'll probably fail for now, and that's all right."

He took the prescription, looked at it as if gazing upon something dear. For a moment, he wanted to cry.

After all these years, he'd found someone who would help him.

Time to start going back to church, he thought.

Dr. Untermann's regal face appraised him, and she smiled. "Have no fear, Mr. Barrows. You've made the first, most crucial step. You've come for help. And *I'll* help you. So many other never do that. We'll see this thing through . . . and fix it."

Barrows felt choked up as he stood. "Thank you . . ." His gaze drifted from her face to the wall behind her, which was covered with degrees and certificates. "You must be . . . pretty good."

"Not to sound pretentious, Mr. Barrows, but as for treating cases such as yours, I'm probably the best in the country. Go home now. Think about what we've discussed, and envision the end of your affliction."

"I will."

"Tomorrow at six, then?"

"Yes . . ."

"And get that prescription filled tonight."

"I will."

She lit another long slim cigarette: long and slim and refined like herself. "Goodnight, Mr. Barrows."

Misty-eyed, Barrows left the office. Part of his psyche, of course, urged him to head right back down to his hunting grounds and search for the strange, tender morsels of his need.

But not tonight.

Because as he made his exit from the frosty, handsome woman's office, he realized he was leaving with something he'd never had in the last two decades.

He was leaving with hope.

It was like heroin. It was like high-grade crack or freshly distilled crystal meth. Extreme obsessive-compulsive disorders affected the same neurotransmitters that the most highly addictive narcotics affected. Marsha. Untermann had seen enough victims to know not only this but the ultimate implications.

You always start a patient off with a positive purview—that was essential—but the rest was never easy. Sometimes it was impossible, and Dr. Untermann knew impossible when she saw it.

She knew that Barrows wouldn't make it.

Her black Bally high heels clicked along the clean cement of the parking garage beneath the twenty-story mirror-faceted Millennium Tower, and it was a nice, new black Mercedes 450 that she slid into. She lit another cigarette—a beastly habit, she knew—but didn't yet start the engine and leave for her lakeside Fremont condo. Instead . . .

She thought.

Extreme obsessive-compulsive disorders–OCD's? Especially the really radical ones?

The trichotillomanics, the aphasics, the dysgeusaics? The success rate was actually so low, it was scarcely worth treatment. It was actually less than the seven-percent success-rate for crack addicts. Much less.

The same went for the disorders akin to dritiphily.

Dr. Untermann had learned much in her nearly thirty years of abnormal clinical psychiatry. She'd learned that some things weren't worth trying to treat.

She heard the footsteps even before the figure turned the corner. She powered down the driver's side window.

"I got a lot this time," a sand-papery voice told her.

"I'm pleased."

Dirty hands passed in the parcel. Untermann took it and handed the figure a $100 bill. "Thank you," she said. "See you tomorrow."

Her purveyor said nothing in response. He simply took the money and walked away. The back of his coat read KING STREET GOSPEL HOMELESS SHELTER.

Untermann gave a hot sigh when she opened the parcel: a paper bag containing a plastic Zip-Loc bag, the one-gallon size. She unzipped the bag, inhaled the aroma, and nearly swooned; the bag was heavy with various vomit. Gritty. Fuming.

Like chunky pink oatmeal.

No, some things weren't worth trying to treat. But capitulation was a treatment of its own, wasn't it? Sometimes you just had to surrender to the incontrovertible truth.

Be who you are, she thought in the ultimate Freudian nod. She flicked out her cigarette. *Accept it, and adapt.*

That's what *she* had done. And it worked. The verity of the soul, however unseemly at times, must always be embraced. Not ignored or fought against.

Embraced.

And now this fox financier, this man Barrows. Smart, successful, rich. And more than pleasing to the eye. When Barrows learned that there really was no cure for his disease, he, too, would capitulate . . . and the two of them would embrace *each other*.

Her nipples suddenly stood out beneath the lacy cotton bra and sheer Biagiotti cashmere blouse. Her sex moistened; her teeth ground. In her mind, she saw Barrows forlornly straying the city's most malodorous streets and alleyways, searching for those all-too-precious nuggets, scraping them up and sucking them down like so many melted diamonds. She saw his trembling lips jacked needily open as unwashed derelicts and dirty, wan whores hacked up veritable collops of meaty phlegm into his mouth. His own uniqueness was all too similar to Untermann's own.

I'll show him how to adapt, just as I have adapted . . .

I'll teach him how to function, unscathed.

We'll be who we both really are. Not in social fallacy but in truth.

Two human beings one in the same.

Together.

Dr. Untermann finally started the car and drove out of the parking garage. The bag sat beside her in the fine leather passenger seat. She couldn't wait to get home—

Oh, yes . . .

—to eat.

Makak

Casparza was repulsive—a human blob. He couldn't pack the food into his fat face fast enough. *Look at him*, Hull thought, disgusted. *Just another greasy spic blimp.*

But the girl—she was beautiful, and all class. She'd said her name was Janice. *Too old to be squeeze*, Hull decided. *Mid or late-twenties.* He'd heard all the stories; the fat man was a kiddie-diddler—anything over 15 was over the hill. So how did Janice figure into it? She looked like a typical American businesswoman. Come to think of it, Hull had seen lots of Americans milling about the plush villa. What were so many Americans doing *here*? This was Peru.

And the black guy? Hull had noticed him at once. Weird. The guy was just standing there off by some trees. *What is this? Some voodoo fucking freak show*? Hull thought. The guy had dreadlocks past his shoulders, and he was wearing some dashiki-looking thing with something hanging off the sash. Hull had never seen a black man so black. Like anthracite. And the guy hadn't moved. He just stared at them from afar, blank-faced.

"So, Mr. Hull," Casparza bid. "This is most irregular. We rarely deal direct, especially small-timers. But I know some of your people. They say good of you."

That's nice to hear, you fat shit.

Casparza weighed 400 pounds plus. The grinning face scarcely appeared human—comic features pressed into dough. He wore a preposterous white straw hat, and pants and a shirt that could tarp a baby elephant.

"The goddamn DEA interdictions are killing us," Hull informed him.

"They're killing the major cartels too," Janice pointed out. Her voice seemed reserved, hushed. Perhaps she was Casparza's spokeswoman. She had straight, pretty ash blond hair and wore a rather conservative beige business dress. A tiny pendant hung about her neck, but Hull couldn't make it out. She primly held a lit cigarette, though he had yet to see her take a drag. She hadn't eaten, either. The servants had brought food only to Hull and Casparza: some brown mush called *aji*, a stinky napalm-hot fish stew, and slabs of something the fat man had merely referred to as "meatroll! My favoreet!" Dessert had been *anticoucho*, collops of fried sheep heart on sticks.

Hull hadn't eaten much.

"And now my amigo would like to buy from me," Casparza went on. His accent hung thick as the rolls of flab descending his chest.

"That's right, Mr. Casparza. Our middlemen are getting blanked out. The Bolivians can't be trusted, and the Colombians are losing 80 percent of their orders to seizures. My whole region is going nuts."

Which was an understatement. Peru had been the number three producer; now it was number one. After the hostage thing, the Tactical Air Command had clobbered the Colombian strongholds and Agent Oranged a hundred thousand acres of their best coca fields, and now there was talk of dropping a light infantry division into Bolivia. This was bad for business; Hull had money to make and customers to please. He needed ten keys a month to keep his region happy, but now he was lucky to see two. The fucking feds were ruining everything. He'd had no choice but to come to see Casparza in person. The fat man had a secret.

"You guarantee delivery," Hull said. "Nobody else does that.

You've become a bit of a legend in the states. Word is you haven't lost a single drop to the feds."

"This is true, Mr. Hull." Casparza's huge blackhole mouth opened wide and sucked a piece of sheep heart off a skewer. It crunched like nuts when he chewed. "But my production surplus is no very good."

"The influx of orders is maxing us out," Janice coolly added.

"I understand that." Hull trained his attentions on Casparza, though the girl's strait-laced beauty nagged at him. At first he thought the pendant around her neck was a locket; closer peripheral inspection showed him a tiny bag of something, or a tied pouch. *She's probably some whacked out New Ager from California,* Hull snidely considered. He *hated* California. *It's probably a pouch full of crystal dust or some shit, to purify her fucking aura.* But of course that didn't mesh with the rest of her looks--primo, neat as a pin. And there was something about her eyes--just . . . something. "We're a small operation, Mr. Casparza. I only want to buy ten keys a month."

"You know my price?"

"Yes," Hull said. Goddamn right he did. The drug war had jacked prices through the roof. A year ago a kilo of "product" ran for 13.5 a key. Now they wanted 25. Casparza charged 30 and he got it. Nobody knew how he evaded seizure losses, and nobody cared. They just wanted the fat man's shit. Even at 30k per drop the profit margin remained huge considering street value and higher pocket prices. But Casparza was a millionaire. He needed Hull's penny-ante business like he needed another helping of meatroll.

"I can pay 35 a key," Hull finally said. The offer would be taken either as a compliment or a grievous insult. Hull knocked on the table leg.

"Hmmm," Casparza remarked. "Let me think. I think better when I eat."

You must think a lot, ya tub of shit.

Sunlight dappled the huge table through plush trees. Hull could smell the fresh scents of the jungle. He looked at Janice again. Yes, it was a tiny pouch at the end of her necklace. She smiled meekly, but her eyes did not match.

"You remind me of home," she said.

"Where's that?"

She didn't reply. Her eyes seemed to beseech him, yet her face remained composed. Hull thought he could guess her story; a lot of the cartel honchos paid big bucks for white girls. Was that what her eyes were saying? *Her eyes*, Hull thought. They looked sad, extant.

Casparza shoveled more fried meat into his face, then chugged down a third tumbler of yarch, which smelled liked sewer water but didn't taste half bad. Hull craned around; the black guy in the dashiki was still standing off by the trees. He couldn't be a bodyguard; he was a stick. Besides, Casparza had more guns than the White House. The black guy hadn't moved in an hour.

"Who's the shadow?" Hull eventually asked.

"Raka," Casparza grunted, cheeks stuffed.

"Mr. Casparza's spiritual advisor," Janice augmented. *Spiritual advisor, my cock*, Hull thought. He didn't believe in spirit. He believed in the body and what the body demanded of the lost. He believed in the simple objectivities of supply and demand. Spirit could go fuck itself. Splrit was bad for business.

"Raka is from Africa, the Shaniki province." Casparza wiped his fat fingers on the tablecloth. "He helps me. He is my guiding light."

You need a guiding light, dumbo. You're so fat you block out the sun.

Hull squinted. The black unresponsive face stared back unblinking. Was he staring at Hull, or *through* him? The braided dreadlocks dangled like whipcords. Hull still couldn't identify the thing that hung off Raka's sash.

Casparza chuckled, jowls jiggling. "You are wondering how I do it, yes? You are wondering how it is that I lose no product while everyone else loses their ass."

Sure, blubberhead. I'm wondering. "That's your affair, Mr. Casparza. I'm just a businessman trying to stay afloat."

Casparza's grin drew seams into his immense face. "Truth is power, and spirit is truth. Think about that, amigo. Think hard."

Hull knew shit when he smelled it. Were they playing with him? The black guy watching his back and Casparza's grinning, porky face in front was about all Hull's nerves could stand. But just as he became convinced that this whole thing was a mistake, Casparza stood up, his shadow engulfing the table. He offered his fat hand.

"We have a deal, Mr. Hull. Ten keys a month at 35 a key. "

Hull jumped up. He shook the fat man's hand, suppressing the abrupt gust of relief. "I can't thank you enough, Mr. Casparza. It's an honor to do business with you."

"Just remember what I said," the fat grin beamed, "about spirit."

Hull could think of no response.

Casparza laughed. His eyeballs looked like marbles sunk in fat. "We make arrangements in the morning. Until then, make yourself at home."

"Thank you, sir."

"Janice will show you around."

The fat man lumbered off. He'd been sitting on a packing crate— Hull noticed now—since no chair on earth could accommodate his girth. Rolls of fat hung off his sides and wriggled like jello.

"Ready for the 25¢ tour?" Janice inquired.

"Sure," Hull said. He was elated. He'd done it; he'd made his deal. But impulse dragged at his gaze. Hull turned his head in tingling slowness.

Raka, the black shadow, was gone.

"You're either very stupid or very desperate," Janice said. She led him past the pool. Several girls—blondes—frolicked nude in the water, while a few more lay back in lounge chairs, taking turns freebasing. None of them could have been older than 16.

"I'm probably a little bit of both," Hull answered her. "But what makes you think so?"

Janice lit a cigarette. "You've got balls coming down here. Alone. An independent with a small order."

Hearing this prim and proper woman say *balls* was oddly erotic. "I've got a business to run," Hull pointed out. "A direct deal was my last resort. You wouldn't believe what the states are like since the crackdown. I hate to think how many times I've driven around all night with a suitcase full of hundreds and no one to give it to. But your boss guarantees delivery. I had to give it a shot."

Now the girls who'd been freebasing lay back in grinning stupors. Two more climbed out of the pool for their turns, one so young she scarcely had pubic hair. Hull did not feel even abstractly responsible. Loss was always someone else's gain. Why shouldn't he be in on it? He was just a purveyor to a need. *Supply and demand, kids. It's not my fault the world's a piece of shit. If I don't sell it, somebody else will.*

One of the blondes smiled at him, her white legs spread unabashed on the lounge chair. A blowjob maybe, but there was no way Hull would want to fuck any of the pool girls. Too young; kids weren't his style. *See?* he thought, a comical testament to God. *I've got morals.* A drug marketeer, Hull was no stranger to lots of sex; he liked nothing more than breaking a couple of nuts per day into a nice, hot box. But *seasoned* women were more his bag. Women with experience. Women who knew themselves, and were sure of themselves. Like—

Well, like his escort, for instance.

He tried to catch glimpses of Janice as she led him out of the court. Great figure, great legs. Not age but more like a refinement had crept into her model's face, tightening the mouth, etching tiny lines at the corners of the eyes. *Her eyes*, he contemplated again. They were probably once very beautiful. Now they looked lackluster. How long ago had *she* been one of the girls in the pool? Her eyes showed all the broken pieces of her dreams, but Hull didn't feel particularly guilty about that, either. Why should he? He wouldn't mind fucking her, though—no, indeed. That would be nice, wouldn't it? Humping a good one off up her slot. He could imagine it in his mind: wet and ready, and a gorgeous dark-blond thatch. Then maybe he'd turn her around and treat her to a second load up the back door. *Hmmm.* A nice thought, at least. He was probably even entitled to now that he was Casparza's client.

But what the hell was that goddamn little thing around her neck?

She took him down the hill. As before she ignored the lit cigarette in her hand. "Here're the works," she said.

Casparza ran an impressive operation. This was no cokehole in the jungle; it was a *complex.* Whole warehouses were devoted to maturation and wash-trenches. Dump trucks one after another roared down from the fields, their beds stacked high with coca leaves. Processors in more warehouses treated and pulped the leaves to new paste. Further treatment and desiccation reduced the paste to purified powder, which would then be distilled to crack once it got to the point people in the States.

Then they passed the camp.

At first Hull thought it must be where the field laborers slept. Rows of camouflaged tents lined the field. In the middle of it all stood a single, much larger tent.

Hull spied several men in business suits walking down the tent rows. They were Americans, obviously.

"What's with all the Americans here?"

"Don't worry about it," Janice told him.

A pair of bent laborers dragged big plastic garbage cans out of the central tent. They disappeared around the side. Standing at the tent's posted entrance was Raka, the black.

"Okay, what's with him, then? What's Raka's story."

"You ask too many questions, Mr. Hull."

I guess I'll take that as a hint. Hull felt entrenched by the sudden weirdness. Americans in business suits? Some black stoneface in a mojo costume? This was a coke factory in the middle of Peru. But the girl was right; he mustn't make waves. *Don't look a gift blimp in the mouth.* As long as Hull got his order, Casparza could have his mystery. He could have his truth and this power and his spirit.

The tour was over. Evening came early here; the jungle darkened in dusk. "I'm impressed," Hull admitted.

"You should be."

Hull kept looking at the camp. More men in suits filed out of the big tent. He saw women, too, dressed like Janice. All clearly Americans.

"Don't worry about it," Janice repeated. It sounded like a warning. "The world is more diverse than we think, Mr. Hull. It's really not a world at all, but a whole bunch of worlds."

"Meaning?"

"This—this place here—is not *your* world."

Hull stared at her.

"Just remember what Casparza said, Mr. Hull. Remember it well."

Her cigarette had grown an inch of ash. Hull's eyes darted from the pendant at her bust to her eyes, always back to her eyes. For a fractured moment he felt seized, or rather bound. He felt tied up by his own confusion. *Her eyes*, he pondered. There was something about her eyes.

Her eyes looked dead.

Janice fingered the makak; it seemed to give off heat.

But Janice felt cold.

She raised her nightgown and rubbed the jelly into her sex. K-Y, the tube read. She barely felt it. The night air steamed around her, but she barely felt that either. She did not sweat. She looked at her hand and saw the cigarette burns encrusted between her fingers.

Moonlight eddied in through the window. Hull lay asleep on the bed. Janice drifted in, still not sure what she was doing. So much was instinct now--habits that sat perched behind her life like ghosts. She envied Hull in his sleep. *Real sleep,* she thought.

Hull reminded her of home, whatever that was. He reminded her of life.

"Mr. Hull?" she whispered, leaning over his bed. She shook him gently. *What am I doing?* she wondered. *Why am I here?*

Hull stirred, then his eyes snapped open. "What . . . ?" he murmured. A pause ticked like dripping wax. Then: "Janice?"

She queried him with her eyes, as if viewing not a person but a notion or an idea only partially interpretable.

"Come here," he said.

She pulled the sheet off and lay beside him. What could she say? I'm lonely, Mr. Hull? You remind me of things? Her fingers closed around his penis. It grew stiff at once. The reaction pleased her; it made her happy: flesh coming to life at her touch. She flinched when he kissed her. His hands felt her body through the nightgown. Again, she wondered if it was the memory of being touched that registered, or the actual sensation. It was like being touched by a ghost.

"You remind me of things," she whispered.

"What things? Tell me."

Janice wanted to cry. Possibly she was, though tearlessly. She hitched her nightgown up and straddled him. His penis slipped right into her sex--another ghost.

He reached for the nightgown. "Take this off."

"No!" she said too quickly.

"You're a beautiful woman, Janice. I want to see you."

Beautiful. Woman. See you. But she didn't want him to see her. She instead pushed the straps off her shoulders and let the gown slide down to her waist. He began to pump slowly in and out. The makak bobbled between her breasts.

"Christ, your pussy feels good," he panted. But even this crude remark pleased her, complimented her. *My pussy feels goood.* It

84

made her feel real.

"I'm gonna come so much in you . . ."

Come. Sperm. Fucking. *Yes, you remind me of things.* What, though? She could remember only in snatches. Each thrust of his penis into her sex pushed a little piece to the surface of her mind. How old had she been? 14? 15? Not an uncommon story. Her father had sodomized her for years. Then she'd run away only to be sodomized by worse people, but by then the drugs held the reins of her life so she didn't really care. She'd been passed back and forth--for anything. Lots of gang bangs and bondage. Lots of fletching. Many times, her man--his name was 'Rome--brought her up for what he called the "Champagne Special." She'd have to blow a roomful of men, spitting each ejaculation into a champagne glass; upon completion, of course, she'd then consume the contents of the glass in one gulp. Dog shows were another regular entertainment for 'Rome's dealer friends. Some of the dogs they brought up were quite large and frisky. "Make Fido happy, Janice," 'Rome had ordered, "or it's no froggie for you." The little white rocks were all the motivation she needed, her treasure at the end of the rainbow, day in, day out. Eventually she'd been sold.

And ended up here.

She'd been sold to Casparza as part of a favor. Casparza liked them young, before they got too beat. He owned many girls. He was too fat to effectively have intercourse, but he liked blowjobs and handjobs. He'd lie on his back and hold his massive belly up as the girls took turns. He also liked tongue baths. "Ah, my little lovers," he'd mutter while several girls slowly licked the greasy sweat off his entire lardacious carriage. Casparza didn't wash much, which made it worse. Sometimes he'd lie on his belly, two girls holding apart his buttocks as others licked his testicles and anus. Occasionally he would defecate on a girl's chest--a squatting human whale--and it always seemed to be poor Janice who received the privilege of eating the spicy excrement.

Once a girl got old—20 or so—he didn't want them anymore. Many were given to the merc camps that patrolled the fields, others simply disappeared. But the lucky ones were saved for special duties. For Raka.

Raka, she thought, riding up and down.

Hull's rhythm steepened. "You are one hot box, Janice—Christ." Her sex made a wet, crinkly noise, like someone eating food. The sensation of motion, of heat and impact, made Janice feel dully elated. Being penetrated—now—was a transposition of sorts, a crossing of matrixes. It put flesh on her memory, life in the space where her heart used to be.

Hull groped for her; he pulled her down, hugging her, as he ejaculated. She could feel his semen spurt into her sex. It felt warm. It was a warm gift he'd given to her, a deposit from one world to another.

She lay back beside him. His finger traced around her breast, then tapped the makak. "What's this?"

My life, she wished she could say. "Just a good luck charm."

"Superstitious, huh? I've seen a lot of people around here with these things. At that camp. What is that place, anyway?" When she didn't answer, he pushed her back. "Let me go down on you. I want to eat your snatch."

"No!" she objected.

He pulled at the nightgown rumpled about her waist.

"No!" she said, grabbing his hands. "Please don't."

"You don't have anything to be self-conscious about."

"Just . . . please . . . don't."

Hull let it rest. He was an attractive man, unabashed in nakedness. He looked clean-cut and professional. He didn't look like what he was, and she supposed that's why Casparza liked him.

"How does he do it?" Hull asked her.

"Do what?"

"How does Casparza get his shit out? He can't be doing it with boats; the U.S. Navy's all over the coast. And surveillance planes are IRing the major land routes 24 hours a day."

"He mules the orders."

Hull leaned up, astonished. "What, commercial air flights?"

"Yes."

"That's *crazy*. Customs checks every plane inside and out, and they fluoroscope and sniff every single piece of luggage and hand-carry on every flight. Casparza's probably moving a thousand keys a month. He can't possibly be muling through airports, not in this day and age. He'd lose everything."

"Just don't worry about it," she wearied. Her hand returned to his penis; it was hard again in moments, hard and hot and pulsing with life. "Do it to me again," she said. "Yeah," he said. "I'll do it to you, all right. You'll like it." He turned her over, pushed her on her belly, and spat between her buttocks. Yet another memory, not surprising. Then he plugged his penis into her rectum, humping her hard.

'Rome, Daddy, all those other men—no big deal. It made her feel good because it reminded her of things.

She hung partway off the bed. The moon seemed to bob up and down in the window with Hull's frenetic thrusts. Janice's hair tossed; the makak danced dangling about her neck. Each impact beat more memories into her head, more life. The ferocious seemed to verify something to her. *This is what people do*, she mused. Hull's penis was proof of life. She wanted him to come in her again; she wished he could come in her forever, for every time he did was another validation that she was something more than a shadow, more than a ghost.

He shuddered, moaning. Janice felt happy. The warm spurts felt thinner and hotter this time, spurtling into her bowel, and she was so happy she wanted to cry. But then—

—she froze.

The face bled into her—black as obsidian and utterly blank. Raka's face.

The priest's voice, an echoic chord, marched across her mind. Now, it commanded.

Still penetrated, Janice slammed the lamp down on Hull's head.

The warped words oozed, spreading. *Truth is power. Spirit is truth.*

The mist of Hull's consciousness trickled up into the light. His eyes lolled open. Blurred faces hovered like blobs, then sharpened, gazing down. Janice and Casparza. He'd been fucking the girl, hadn't he? Yes, and then . . . then . . .

Goddamn, he thought when the rest of the memory landed.

He tried to get up but he couldn't.

"Ah, Mr. Hull." Casparza's face loomed. "Welcome back, amigo."

Hull glanced around. The fuckers had tied him down to a table. He was nude. The hissing light from a dozen gas lanterns licked about drab canvas walls. *The camp,* he realized. *The tent.*

He was in the big tent.

Janice stood beside the table, wan in her nightgown. Casparza stood opposed, the avalanche of flab straining against his huge shirt.

Standing by a canvas partition was Raka.

"We gain power through spirit, Mr. Hull," Casparza cryptified. "Raka is an Obeah priest, a Papaloi. He was bred to harness the spirit."

The black priest stood in total lack of movement, the staring face bereft of life as a wooden mask. He wore a necklace of human fingers, or perhaps pudenda, and the thing that hung from his sash was a shrunken baby's head. But from his hand something else depended, swaying: one of those little bags on a cord, one of the makak.

"I thought we had a deal," Hull moaned.

"Oh, we do, Mr. Hull," the fat man assured. "But you want to know my secret, don't you?"

"I don't give a fuck about your secret. Just let me loose."

"In time." Casparza's grin seemed to prop up the bulbous face. He nodded to Janice.

I'm fucked, Hull realized. He squirmed against his bonds. It didn't take a genius to deduce that they were going to kill him. But why? He hadn't crossed any lines. It didn't make sense. Had some new mover back home put a contract on him? Had someone fingered him as a stool?

"Look, I don't know what I've done, and I don't know what's going on. Just let me go. I'll pay you whatever you want."

Casparza laughed, fat jiggling.

Janice pushed in a wheeled table like a gurney. *Holy motherfucking shit*, Hull thought, and it was the palest of thoughts, and the least human. His eyes felt stapled open. On the gurney lay a corpse: a man, an American. It was pale and naked.

"Janice will show you," Casparza said. "The power of spirit."

Hull grit his teeth. Janice very deftly slit open the cadaver's belly with heavy-gauge autopsy scalpel. She plunged her hands into the rive and began to pull things out. First came glistening pink rolls of intestines, then the kidneys, the liver, stomach, spleen. She tossed each wet mass of organs into a big plastic garbage can. Then she reached up further for the higher stuff--the heart, the lungs. It all went into the can. By the time she was done, she was slick to the elbows with dark, oxygen-starved blood.

"We can fit six or eight keys into the average corpse," Casparza informed.

Hull frowned in spite of his dilemma. "You're out of your mind. That's the oldest trick in the book. Customs has been wise to it for years."

Casparza smiled. Now Janice was packing sealed keys into the corpse's evacuated body cavity, then stuffed in wads of foam rubber to fill in the gaps and smooth things out. She worked with calm efficiency. Finished, she began to sew up the gaping seam with black autopsy suture.

"You can't smuggle coke into the states in cadavers," Hull objected. "Customs inspects all air freight, including coffins, including bodies tagged for transport. Any idiot knows that. The girl said you were muling the stuff."

"That's correct, Mr. Hull. My mules walk right past your customs agents."

Wha—, Hull thought. *Walk?*

Janice raised her nightgown. Hull's eyes, in dreadful assessment, roved up her legs, over the patch of pubic hair, and stopped. Across her belly was a long black-stitched seam.

"Janice has been muling for me for quite some time."

My God, was about all Hull could think.

Raka began muttering something, heavy incomprehensible words like a chant. The words seemed palpable, they seemed to thicken amid the air as fog. They seemed alive. Then he placed one of the makak about the corpse's neck.

And the corpse sat up and climbed off the gurney.

My God, my God, my—

Raka led the corpse out.

Casparza held out his fat hands, his face, for the first time, placid in some solemn knowledge. "So you see, amigo, we still have a deal. And you'll get to be your own mule."

Aw, Jesus, Jesus—

The scalpel flashed splotchily in Janice's hand. Hull began to scream as she began to cut.

The Mother

My God, Smith thought. *This is my wife.*

He'd lain her out naked across the bed. Her nipples looked like bruises now, and her skin—every inch of which he'd once caressed in love—glittered pastily beneath the gelid sweat of death.

My . . . wife . . .

The bivalving scalpel flashed in his hand.

I'm autopsying my wife.

Smith took a heavy breath. Then he began to cut.

"Jeannie! Don't go near that!" Smith shouted. He clambered clumsily after her down the wooded hill, careful of stumps and roots hidden under leaves. Whatever that thing was in the ravine--*A keg?* he wondered. *A drum?*—it just looked . . . nasty. It wasn't supposed to be there, and he didn't want his daughter touching it. "Jeannie!" he shouted once more.

Jeannie gladly pretended not to hear these heated commands of her father, as would most 7-year-olds. Instead she nimbly wended through branches and brush, and descended into the ravine.

The thicket crunched beneath Smith's plodding feet. Two decades of a pack of Parliments a day reminded him how out of shape he was. Some doctor, but at least *his* patients couldn't accuse him of hypocrisies. He loped ahead, gasping, and raised his arms to shield himself from the spiny branches that seemed determined to thwart his progress. Smith was a liberal; he was also an over-reactor. He remembered any number of headlines detailing his worst ecological fears. WAYNESVILLE CANCER RATES FOUND TO BE THREE TIMES HIGHER THAN NATIONAL AVERAGE. A.A. COUNTY FINED MILLIONS FOR SECRETLY PUMPING UNTREATED SEWAGE INTO BAY. BROCK CLIFFS NUCLEAR WASTE WATER SEEPS INTO RESERVOIR. And so on. Smith, as a father, felt legitimately paranoid of the faux pas of this new age of progress. Just nights ago he'd read in the Post about containers of toxic waste that had fallen off a truck near an Edgewood elementary school. Some teenagers had opened one of the containers, and had died in hours. Then there was that town up north, an entire community evacuated when cable tv diggers had uncovered a secretly buried consignment of binary waste products, compliments of the U.S. Army Chemical Corps. The stuff had been there twenty years. No wonder the town's miscarriage and birth defect rates had been so high . . .

What a world, Smith considered

And this thing in the ravine, it looked like a chemical drum of some sort, with bright red stripes like a warning. Smith had spotted it from the back porch with his binoculars. *Bird watching,* he always told Marie. *Oh, that's nice, dear*, she'd said once. *It's wonderful that you haven't lost interest in your childhood hobbies.* This was partly true at any rate; Smith had indeed been an avid bird-watcher as a child. The only thing he watched now, however, was that Donna Whatshername next door, the neighbor's kid. On days she didn't have classes at the community college, she'd lie out in her backyard, to work on her tan. What she also worked on was Smith's libido. *Jeeeeeeesus Christ!* he must've thought a million times, focusing the Bushnell 7x12s. It astounded him, the level to which modern swimwear had reverted. Bikinis these days made the ones Marie had worn years ago look like winter parkas. Smith had a funny feeling that Donna Whatshername knew he was watching her. The poses seemed staged, lewd, nearly masturbatory. Too often the girl would untie her top and idly roll toward Smith's gaze, her eyes closed as if sleepy. Donna was, to put it eloquently, well-possessed of an ample mammarian carriage, or, in Smith's less eloquent consensus: *Good Christ and Lord Almighty, that is one humdinger of a rack of milk wagons!*

All of which had fairly little to do with the bizarre white drum that sat not 100 hundred yards beyond his property line. He'd been focusing up, the usual ritual upon coming home from work, while Marie prepared dinner. Donna sauntered across her own yard as if on cue, all long tan legs, curvy contours, and . . . mammarian carriage.

"Jeeeeeeesus Christ!" Smith muttered, the binoculars close to welded to his eyes. "She ain't wearing a bikini, she's wearing dental floss."

"What's that, dear?"

Smith jerked the Bushnells quickly toward the woods. Marie had come out onto the patio, looking domestic as ever in her fuzzy slippers, lilac sundress, and calico apron.

"A black-throated blue warbler," Smith feigned enthusiasm. "A female too. You can tell by the pink spot on each wing. They're rare for this area."

"Oh, that's nice, dear." Her broad, pretty face shifted in a blink of fuddlement. "I could have sworn you said something about dental floss . . . Anyway, dinner'll be ready in ten minutes. Have you seen Jeannie?"

"Naw," Smith replied, never veering his gaze from the scape of the woods. "She's probably watching those *Star Trek* reruns, as usual. Either that or she's in her room playing with her Kirk and Spock dolls."

Marie disappeared back to the kitchen, leaving Smith slightly asweat. *Be careful, you idiot.* Yes, he'd have to be more careful than this. He felt no shame in his frequent voyeurisms—*Looking's not cheating*, he rationalized. It wasn't like he was having sex with

93

Donna, was it? He was merely reveling in the visual appreciation of her womanhood. What was wrong with that? This was no different than bird watching, espying pretty things in nature, celebrating them. Donna Dental Floss was a rare black-throated blue warbler and nothing more.

But, boy, oh boy, a thought seeped. *What I wouldn't give to—*

The most adulterous images betrayed him. Smith humping the foxy coed hell for leather right there in the grass, his eyes crossed. Dog-style, missionary, her feet pinned back behind her ears—it didn't matter—redepositing one allotment of his semen after the next—

Stop it! he commanded himself. *Don't be a cad!*

But cad or not, just as Smith would turn the binoculars back to the bikini-clad human masterpiece in the next yard, he caught one last glimpse of the wood's descent, and he noticed the—

"What the hell—"

—white, red-striped drum.

"—is that?"

The drum sat half-buried in the ravine, and that's when Smith dropped the Bushnells and bolted, for it wasn't only the white drum that he'd seen, but also his 7-year-old silken haired daughter eagerly ambling toward it.

"Stay AWAY from that! Smith's voice cracked through the dense green woods. Jeannie glanced up, and froze. Terror bloomed in the big, bright-blue eyes. Curiosity incarnate had been caught; Daddy the Destroyer was here.

"One more step, young lady, and you lose your dolls for a week," Smith threatened from the edge of the dried ravine.

"But, Daddy—"

"For a *month,*" he embellished. "Now step away from that thing. It's dangerous. It's dirty."

"No it's not, Daddy," the little girl replied. "It's—"

94

"If you don't do as you're told, missy, it's no more *Star Trek Forever.*"

This horrifying consequence reflected an even deeper terror in Jeannie's shining child-eyes. She paused, peering at the white drum, then backed off. She ascended the ravine's thatchy slope while Smith himself went down. "Stay there," he said, pointing a stern finger.

"But why is it dirty, Daddy?"

"It just is," came his articulate response. He plodded toward the cryptic keg. *How can you explain something like this to a 7-year-old? Well, you see, honey, some really bad man decided to dump this drum of tumor-accelerating, carcinogenic, ganglionic-response-inhibiting and probably irradiated toxic effluvium in our back yard because he was too lazy to dispose of it properly. And it's dirty, dirty stuff, and that means if you get near it your orbital lobes will turn into giant coaxial metastatic masses by the time you're out of college, and your ovaries'll be glowing like a pair of fucking Christmas tree lights.* "It's dirty, honey," he replied instead. "It's like dog poo. You don't want to get near it."

Her little face looked cruxed. "But you're getting near it."

Smith frowned, choosing a long fallen limb. "That's because I'm a grownup, and grownups are allowed. But little girls aren't."

"That's dumb, Daddy," came Jeannie's haughty response.

Precocious, Smith thought. The drum, he saw now, had no writing on it, just the bright-scarlet stripes, which made sense. *If you're going to dump hazardous waste illegally, you don't leave your name and address.* And he was sure now that's what it was. The drum sat on its side as if dropped. At once Smith noticed a meaty scent . . .

Like rotten pork, he thought. His nostrils cringed. Or like that cadaver the county cops brought in last summer. It had ripened in the heat for days, hidden beneath humid hay bales. Cooking.

The drum's rim appeared crimped, offering a small egress. Smith poked the branch into it and pushed. "Aw, shit!" he exclaimed and leapt back. The lid popped off, emptying a gush of black, lumpy sludge into the ravine's craw. Smith could've vomited. The stuff stank worse than a fish market dumpster in high summer.

He gaped at it a moment, his handkerchief to his face. The sludge looked coagulated, like gravy that hadn't evened. Large bubbles rose from the surface of the spill, percolating, and the stench thickened. Thank God the creek had long-since dried up, otherwise the stream would be hauling this gunk away right now. Smith felt momentarily weird, staring at the crisp, popping bubbles. His sweat rushed—the mass of ichor seemed to waft shifts of heat.

"Come on." Smith huffed back up the hillock and led Jeannie away from the ravine. He took long strides, yanking her by the hand. *Boy, this pisses me off,* he fumed. *I've got a kid for God's sake. Some chemical company asshole dumps this crap near kids? Yeah, what a world.*

"I saw a falling star, Daddy," Jeannie remarked as they headed back to Smith's cedar-shingled Colonial. It cost 150k, in a nice culdesac. Smith worked hard for it, and for everything to keep his family comfortable, and then some thoughtless creep pulls a stunt like this. *Word gets around and the whole community could go to hell.* Smith envisioned the headlines. TOXIC WASTE DUMPED IN STORYBOOK TOWN. PROPERTY VALUES PLUMMET. *Assholes*, he thought. "What did you say, honey?"

"But it wasn't really a star," she enlivened on. "It was that drum. I saw it last night."

"You saw *Star Trek* last night is what you saw, miss." *Kids*, Smith thought. Then they were back at the house, back to normality. "Dinner's ready," he said. "Don't forget to wash your hands."

He'd reported the incident to the police anonymously; he didn't need a slew of questions. *With my luck they'll think I had something to do with it.* Smith reasoned that whoever had dumped the sludge had brought it down the old logging road on the other side of the treebelt, and that's what the authorities would conclude.

That night he slept fitfully, dragged in and out of chasms of dreams. He never had bad dreams; his job had cauterized him since med school. Smith was the county coroner, and after so many years of autopsying human grotesqueries atop his Aimsworth pitch-tilt powerdrain morgue table, he could eat a tuna on rye with one hand and fish through gunshot intestinal vaults with the other. No big deal. Tonight, however, towlines of nightmares hauled him through rank mind-muck visions the likes of which his slumber had never before offered up. "She's eating, Daddy, she's eating! Isn't Mommy pretty when she eats?" Jeannie smiled in her Care Bear pajamas, gazing down into the nighted ravine. Meanwhile, Smith's wife knelt naked at the opened drum. With enthusiasm, she plucked lumps out of the stinking black spillage and sucked them off her fingers. Moonlight shimmered through the trees, a tinseled vertigo. Jeannie's eyes shined wide as brand-new silver dollars. "Eat, Mommy, eat. I'd eat too but I'm too little." Smith wanted to puke in the dream. *Yeah, bend over and let 'er rip.* It was not an easy thing to watch your extremely inhibited wife eat lumps of chemical shit out of a bubbling, odorous mass of toxic waste. No, this was not an easy thing to watch at all. "Oh, it tastes simply scrumptious, dear," Marie remarked. "You really should try some." *No thanks, hon. That stuff's probably not on the Atkins' Diet.* "Daddy can't eat that," Jeannie was quick to relate, which relieved Smith in his dream-paresis. He seemed to be lashed to a tree, forced to watch this disgusting play of nightmare in his boxer shorts. "The Mother," Jeannie kept chanting from the hillock's edge. "The Mother, the Mother." *Freud would shit in his pants if he could see this dream*, Smith managed to muse. He fairly understood the psychology of dreams: eroto-societal symbolism, sex-death links, and all that. But—*Sex-sludge links?* he wondered. What did this scenario say about himself? It came as no surprise when, next, Donna, the lissome neighbor of the dental floss bikinis, traipsed down into the hot ravine. She too was buck naked, and she wasted no time in joining Marie's putrid smorgasbord. "Donna can eat too," Jeannie rejoiced. "It's only Daddy who can't eat, not here." The dream seemed to peel Smith's eyelids off; Freud's manifestos forced him to watch. *Good God,* he thought, aghast. Donna and Marie openly caressed themselves in the lump-laden bilge. They were kissing! "Here," Marie invited. She passed a lump, about the size of a walnut, from her own mouth into Donna's. "More," Donna panted. *Good God,* Smith thought again. *Would somebody PLEASE wake me up!* Marie, lying back in the black scum, had placed more of the lopsided lumps up and down her belly and betwixt her breasts, for Donna to eat off. "Your husband's got a hard one for me," Donna commented between morsels. "Don't get your hopes up," Marie laughed back, caressing herself in the slime. "He comes way too fast, and he's not very big. Sort of like one of those little breakfast links." They cackled at this remark, like witches breathing helium. Smith fumed in spite of his revulsion. *Breakfast link, huh?* "God, this stuff is really boss," Donna delighted. Soon, when she and Smith's wife had sufficiently filled their bellies, they focused their appetites on each other. Smith was sweating. This was like the lesbian porno flicks they'd shown at his bachelor party, only they hadn't included curdled toxic sludge in the production. Donna and Marie slithered over one another in the muck, beslicking their bodies. They shined like black human lacquer. "Isn't this great, Daddy?" Jeannie inquired, clapping with glee in the moonlight. *No,* Smith thought. *This is not great.* "Oooo," Marie cooed. "You do it so much better than my husband." Smith frowned. Donna's face, amid a sound quite similar to that of a big, hungry dog tearing into a pile of Alpo, busied itself between Marie's spread legs . . .

Smith didn't know how much more of this he could take. *Aw, it's only a dream,* he dismissed. "You'll have to eat too, Daddy," his daughter informed him again. "But not here, not at the Mother's." *What the hell are you talking about, you little imp!* Smith thought in a burst of frustration. But then Marie and Donna were drifting up the ravine's slope. Giggling, they took Smith away from the tree and lay him down paralyzed into the sludge. "Not too much," Marie warned as her hands roved her husband's rather flabby chest. "I told you, he comes real fast." Smith frowned again. When he glanced past his burgeoning belly, he noted that Donna was fellating him, and via a considerable level of proficiency. The coed stopped a moment, disengaging her mouth long enough to chuckle and remark, "You're right, Marie, it is like a breakfast link!" This infuriated Smith further. *What, a guy's gotta have a leg of lamb between his legs to keep a woman happy? Christ.* "He's close, you better get on him now," Donna suggested. The sludge crackled as Marie prepared to mount him. But then it was Smith's daughter's face that bulged forward, warped in cherubic youth like a fisheye lens. "No!" the demanding little voice echoed. "Daddy's not ready yet! Daddy has to visit the Father!"

Smith spent the next day at work hungover. At least that's what it felt like, a bezeled drill bit spinning through the pulp of his brain. He'd stopped drinking years ago; he'd opened too many Parke-Davis cadaver bags full of too many mangled drunk drivers, and he'd histologized too many swollen, sclerotic livers too many times. Yet his head pounded all day. Splinters raged behind his eyes.

The dream, he kept thinking. *The nightmare.*

He saw the heinous black wads everywhere: in the autoclave, in the chromatograph receptacle, on the flat top of the Vision Series blood analyzer and in the morgue table's stainless steel runoff gutters. He even saw them in the Polar Water bottle, and in his lunch . . .

But only for an instant.

When he blinked, they were gone.

Backwash, that was all. The nightmare had wrung him out. *Get your act together*, Smith. He'd bungled two y-sections already today, and had to jink the autopsy reports. Thank God Smith's clients could tell no tales. He hadn't been so off the mark in years.

Eventually he dismissed the dream as frivolity, just a lewd

99

mindstage of fear and guilt. Fear that a drum of chemical waste had been dumped behind his house, and guilt from his voyeurism. He felt much better about the whole thing when he called home that afternoon. "The police were out back earlier," Marie related, "and then some cars with EPA seals came. They took the drum away in a big truck. It was like a movie, men in gas masks and white rubber suits were poking around. They sprayed some kind of foam all around the ravine and left notices in everybody's mailbox saying that the area is safe and there's nothing to worry about." This news relieved Smith fully. The white drum was gone now, and its black spillage decontaminated. End of story.

But not end of headache.

When Smith drove home, he spotted Donna walking away from the bus stop. "Need a lift?" he offered.

"Sure, thanks," she replied and slid into Smith's big Buick. Her blond head cocked, though, and she peered at him. "Are you all right, Mr. Smith? You look, like, oh, I don't know, like you're all tensed up or something."

Mr. Smith. Christ, she makes me feel like a dinosaur. "I've had a rip-roaring headache all day, that's all."

"Well, wait, put the car in park," she oddly suggested.

"Why?"

She slid right next to him, smiling. "I'll rub your temples."

Smith blushed. "Uh, well, uh, you know—I'm kind of like, you know . . . Married."

Donna laughed lackadaisically. "Mr. Smith, letting a girl rub your temples isn't exactly what I'd call being unfaithful."

Smith considered this, trying hard not to stare at Donna's cut-offs and orange halter. *Well, uh, yeah, she's right. What's the harm in letting her rub my temples* . . . Smith pulled over, put the Buick in park. "Uh, okay," he said.

"Turn this way, lean back a little," the 19-year-old directed. "That's it, that's good."

Smith leaned back against Donna's formidable bosom, while her thumbs gently massaged his temples. Her breasts felt like firm, plush cushions against his shoulder blades.

Smith's eyes closed on their own. He struggled to make petty conversation. "So, uh, Donna, tell me. How's college?"

"Great," she replied. Rubbing. Rubbing. "How's bird watching?"

Smith gulped. "Uh, uh, great. I saw a black-throated blue, uh, warbler yesterday."

"Mmmmm," she said. Did she chuckle too? Rubbing, still rubbing, she went on, "That's wild about that drum of chemicals they found, isn't it?"

Rubbing. Rubbing.

"Uh, yeah," Smith fairly moaned. "Wild."

Her deft thumbs continued to knead Smith's aching temples. *Christ, I'm getting hard,* he noted of the swelling at his groin. He felt lazed back into the sweetest dream . . .

Her blond hair smelled lovely, like herbs and soap. Then her lips came very close to Smith's ear and she whispered: "Does that feel good, Mr. Smith?"

"Yes," Smith moaned.

"Hmmmm?"

"Yeeeeees.

Her lips moved closer, the hot breath caressing his ear. "Has Mr. Smith been a good boy? Hmmm?"

Aw, Jesus, Smith thought. He felt as paralyzed as he'd felt in the nightmare.

"Hmmm? You can tell Donna, can't you? Has Mr. Smith been a good boy?"

"Uh, uh, uh . . ."

Her thumbs were like mainlines of opium to his brain. Her breath seemed to lick his neck.

"Be a good boy now and tell Donna that you're ready, okay, baby? Are you ready? Have you been a good boy?"

By now Smith could not offer a verbal reply. He moaned some more, and he may have whined. But—

Donna reclined the power seat. As Smith descended, he saw that the coed had removed her orange halter, and his recognition of this fact dripped like slow molasses in his head. *Holy Jesus to fargin' Pete, what a rack of milk wagons . . .*

And indeed they were: large, perfectly symmetrical orbs of flesh, with pert pink nipples.

"Let's get you primed, Mr. Smith," she suggested, giggling. "Let's get this pump good and primed." And with that statement, her hands began to caress his crotch. "Yeah, we're gonna get Mr. Smith all boned up, because Mr. Smith's been a good boy, hasn't he?"

Smith raised no objection whatsoever when, a moment later, she pulled his pants and boxers to his knees. Her fingers caged his testicles, and her mouth went south . . .

Smith wanted to shout: *No! Don't do that! I'm a married man, and I love my wife, and I WILL NOT be unfaithful to her. So you just stop that right now!* In reality, though, he uttered no such thing, electing instead to just lie back and let her proceed. And indeed she did proceed, with hair-raising expertise. "Mmmmm," she kept moaning in her throat. "Mmmmmmmmm." The hot, frictive sensation made him feel electrified: her mouth was a 220-volt wall socket, and Smith's penis was the plug. Her firm-as-grapefruits breasts prodded his thigh as she maintained the slow, excruciating ministration. At one point, Smith gazed down over his paunch, and she gazed up, desisting long enough to remark of his 4-inch erection, "Oh Mr. Smith, it's just so-so--so . . . *big!*"

Smith made a stiff face, recalling the nightmare. *No, it's not. It's a breakfast link, remember?* And he could've sworn that, when she'd made this comment, there'd been an undue hilarity in her eyes. *Look at me*, he thought, self-disgusted. *I'm a successful 39-year-old man, with a great career, a great wife, a great kid—a great life. And what am I doing? I'm getting a blowjob from a blonde teenage sexpot in the front seat of a Buick Regal.* Yet despite this acknowledgement, he was helpless to do anything about it. He was risking everything, wasn't he? If he got caught, he would lose everything he cherished, everything he'd worked so hard for. But Donna was a seductress, a sex-siren. Smith felt that he'd be unable to pull away from this even with a gun to his head. All he could do was simply submit to this harrowing, absolutely mind-wringing oral mastery of hers . . .

And just before Smith would ejaculate—

She stopped.

What the hell are you doing! Smith wanted to bellow. Why on earth had she stopped? Her eyes beseeched him, the sultry face in the frame of fragrant blond hair rose upward. "You've been a good boy, right, Mr. Smith? You're ready, right?"

Smith, infuriated, gasped at the ludicrous question, pointing to his indisputably erect member. "For God's sake, doesn't it *look* like I'm ready?" his voice grated.

She papped his nose with a finger. "That's not what I mean, Mr. Smith." Her lips played at his ear. "What I mean is . . . are you ready?"

The word dropped like a stone in his head.

Ready.

Are you ready?

Smith's memory ticked. The nightmare. Jeannie—

What had Jeannie said in the nightmare?

Something about being . . . ready?

Yes—

Donna's preeminent breasts vised his face. Her fingers weaved through his hair. "Oh, Mr. Smith," she whispered. "Please tell me that you've been a good boy. Please . . . tell me that you're ready."

Ready? Yeah, I was ready, all right, you teasing, fickle bitch, Smith thought, driving the Buick home. How much more ready could he have been? *Cock-tease! Evil cunning slut!* She'd brought him to the brink, then left him hanging like clothes on a line. *She primed my pump, that's for sure—*

Then she'd left. Smith, incredulous, had stared after her as she'd opened the car door, gotten out, and walked away, leaving him with his pants at his knees and his unslaked erection bobbing in his lap. *Women are such evil bitches*, he glumly thought. *Cock-teasing, evil fickle little harlots . . .*

His headache raged when he arrived home. Jeannie lay before the tv in the family room, her little ankles crossed in the air. She raptly watched *Star Trek* reruns. "They stole Spock's brain, Daddy!" she fretted upon his entrance. *Tough luck for Spock*, Smith thought. He remembered the episode. "Don't worry, honey. I think Bones will save the day," he consoled. *How about taking my brain--along with this fucking headache!* "I hope they catch the slobs who dumped that crap," Smith griped to his wife, who tended to dinner at the Jenn-Air range. "I mean, Christ, couldn't they have dumped it in Jersey like everyone else?" "I'm sure they'll catch them, dear," Marie assured. "So why don't you just relax?" When Smith sat down at the table, Marie came around to rub his temples.

"No bird-watching tonight, dear?"

"Naw," Smith said, swallowing his guilt like a lump of phlegm.

"How's that headache?"

"It's—" Then Smith paused. He hadn't told her of his headache, had he? "How did you know I had a headache?"

"Honey—" Rubbing. Rubbing. "You told me this afternoon."

"This afternoon?" Smith questioned.

"This afternoon when you called me. Remember? You called me to ask if anyone had come about the drum, and I told you the police were here, and the EPA men—"

"Yeah, yeah," Smith said. "I remember. Sorry, this headache's killing me. I'm just out of it today."

Out of it was putting it lightly. And Marie's affection, her sheer care for him, made Smith feel even worse now. *Fifteen minutes ago I was letting a blond coed suck my dick, and she didn't even do it long enough for me to come . . . What was wrong with him? The gifts of his life couldn't be more plain. His loving wife, his* lovely little girl, his home. All right, so Marie would never make the cover of *Swimwear Illustrated.* Her breasts, not nearly as large as Donna's, had a bit of droop to them now, and she was getting a trifle wide in the caboose department. But-- She'd stuck with him through thick and thin. She'd given him a beautiful daughter and a beautiful life. She was *real*, and her *love* was real. How could anything else matter? The girl next door was just something pretty, a bird in a sense, a black-throated blue warbler no more real to Smith than the August centerfold of *Penthouse.*

At once his guilt fell down on him, like a mineshaft cave-in.

"Marie?" he peeped.

"Yes, dear?" Rubbing. Rubbing. "What is it?"

Smith was suddenly close to tears. "I-I-I . . ."

"Honey? What is it?"

My God, Smith realized. "I love you."

"I love you too," Marie said.

"No, no, I mean . . ." But what did he mean? "I mean, like, I *really* love you."

Marie's voice seemed to grow hot. Her fingers meandered at his temples. "Why don't you show me?" she whispered.

Fuck dinner, Smith concluded. He led Marie by the hand up the stairs, to the bedroom. He slowly stripped her, reveling at the vision of her body, pale skin and cellulite and crooked teeth and all. "Make love to me, darling," she hotly breathed. She lay back on the bed, parting her thighs. And what she said next absolutely shocked him, for Marie had never been one to talk dirty.

"I want your cock in my pussy, darling. I want you to stick your cock all the way up my pussy and come in me."

The words alone nearly made Smith come, the words in addition to Donna's previous attentions. *Yeah, she primed my pump, all right. But to hell with her. I have a loving wife. I have a real woman . . .*

"Stick your cock in me right up to the balls and come, you big beautiful fucking love-machine. Squirt all that wonderful jizz right up into my little honey hole."

Smith was dizzied. He lay atop her and obliged. At once her hand slithered around and massaged his buttocks. "Come, baby, come," she breathed. "Come in my pussy, darling . . ."

Aw, shit! Smith was going to come, all right. Quite expeditiously. He tried to stave it off, think about baseball, Mantle's 500th homer, which Smith had seen with his dad, Marris breaking Ruth's record, and Catfish Hunter's first 20-win season. Boy, could the Catfish throw a spitter!

But it didn't work. How could it? This was love, not childhood baseball memories.

After a strenuous, sweat-popping five seconds, Smith ejaculated, exhaling like a busted raft. Marie moaned with each pulse, wrapping her legs about his back.

"Oh, honey," Smith nearly wept into the crook of her neck. "I'm sorry, I'm so sorry . . ."

And what a cruel ripoff this was. Smith generally lasted at least half a minute. *Punishment*, he thought; his guilt continued to assail him. Yes, the universe was punishing him for being with Donna, decimating his already less-than-impressive endurance.

"I'm so sorry, Marie . . ."

Her warm hand played over his scalp. "That's all right, dear. I . . . I know."

Smith's heart skipped a beat. *She knows?* he thought in sheer terror. *She knows about Donna?*

But then he simmered down. No, no, she didn't know about that. How could she? She merely meant that she understood Smith's problem with premature ejaculation. She was so understanding, so considerate. *What a woman*, Smith realized, as drenched in shame as he was sweat. But—

Yes!

There was something he could do for her, wasn't there?

Smith slithered down . . .

"Oooo, sweetheart," Marie cooed lewdly. "You know exactly what I want, you dirty little sex-muffin."

Yeah, Smith thought. Here was this wonderful, warm, passionate woman who'd offered herself solely for Smith's pleasure. Now he would return the gesture.

Yeah.

Her white thighs opened before his face like a newspaper. Her fingers raked his hair, while her own hair—her private hair—tickled around Smith's mouth. Suddenly he felt bent on something, frantic in the taste of her. Compelled. Driven.

"That's it, sweetheart, that so good," she breathed. "You do it so good, you big love-tongue, you . . ."

The synchronicity of Smith's tongue against her pleasure quickened in increments; he chased her squirming hips across the bed. Smith kissed, licked, lapped—

"So good, sweetheart—"

Kissed, licked, lapped.

"So good, so good, such a—"

Kissed, licked, lapped.

"—good good boy."

Smith's eyes bulged. A good boy?

Hadn't Donna said the exact same thing . . .

But before he could even reckon such a coincidence, Marie seemed to gasp, and her body seemed to . . . tremor.

Smith's mouth remained locked at her sex when the septic stench rose. Marie gasped again, then her hips twitched, then—

Holy mothherfucking SHIT!

Several hard, steady dolphin spurts of the stinking black sludge shot into his mouth. He wedged away in shock, paused to bend over and vomit, and when he raised his head again, a final pulse of sludge jettisoned right in his face.

Over the rise of her breasts, Marie's eyes fixed on him.

"You didn't, did you?" she gargled.

Smith stared, frozen in disgust.

Marie craned her neck further, her face wavering. "You weren't ready, were you?" she gushed. It sounded like an accusation. "Goddamn you, you were supposed to be ready . . ."

Then her eyes rolled up white, and her head fell back.

Ready, Smith thought. His face dripped. Madness. The silence gaped at him as he tried to bring her back. No pulse. No breath. He straddled her. *One, two, three, four, five,* his thoughts counted off in CPR. With each downward thrust, more black slime eddied from each orifice. Popping black bubbles frothed at her lips, ears, and nostrils. Then the truth slapped him in the face as hard as the insanity of this entire situation:

"She's dead," he whispered.

It was too much, too fast. All rationale escaped him; his psyche felt stuffed, like a Szechuan squid stuffed to bursting. Marie seemed to be on the verge of bursting too. Movement churned beneath her pale, dead belly. Revulsion, shock, etc. cut Smith's spiritual tether, leaving only his objective remains: Smith the Coroner, Smith the Man Who Autopsies Dead People for a Living. It was impulse now, in this moment of intractable impossibility. He went for his old med school bag in the closet, and his old CMS knife set.

Thoughts swarmed but he didn't really hear them. The sharp bivalving blade flashed. "Aw, God," he muttered, cutting. "Aw, no." The incision stretched as he drew the gleaming blade from hip to hip, exuding a goulash of black lumps. She was a doll stuffed with beans. Out they poured as Smith watched, slow black lava sliding over the sides of the bed.

Lumps, he thought. *The drum. The sludge.*

The lumps began to dissolve, reverting to thin dark slime, upon their exposure to the air. They crackled, sputtering. The stench rose like steam from a corpse-pit.

Lumps, he thought. *My wife.*

Dead lumps.

I wasn't a good boy. I wasn't ready.

The door swung open behind him. The thin shadow played across the floor. "Oh, Daddy, now look what you've done!" sniped the irritated little voice of his daughter. "You weren't ready, were you?"

"No," Smith muttered, thinking of the dream. "No, I wasn't. I'm sorry. I wasn't . . . ready."

"Daddy!" She scowled at him, arms crossed in her flannel pajamas. "You've been a *bad* boy."

"I-I know."

"Come on," she huffed. Her little hand led him from the bedroom, down the quiet stairs, and outside. Crickets trilled. Legions of fireflies shifted their tiny lights against a sultry evening. Smith, naked, enslimed, followed Jeannie down the hill behind his house.

The woods, he thought. *The ravine.* But hadn't Marie said that they'd taken the drum away?

"Hurry, Daddy!"

Branches scratched his face and chest but he didn't feel it. Dappled moonlight lit their progress; the forest was a labyrinth. With each step came more and more of some throbbing revelation, like Marie's abdominal wall before Smith had riven it open, and like the throbbing headache.

The ravine lay empty, save for crusts of the decontaminant foam they'd sprayed. Jeannie had to constantly wait up for him, like the time he'd taken her to the mall to see Santa. But it was not Santa that awaited him now. Smith could feel it, drawing on his brain, calling him . . .

The Father, came the strange thought.

"You were supposed to visit the Father first, Daddy. But you didn't. And that's why the Mother's babies died in Mommy."

"Yes," Smith droned.

A hundred yards past the ravine Smith could see it. A drum, identical to the first, save that it was black instead of white. *Black and white*, Smith thought. *Yin and Yang. Mother and Father.*

He gazed down.

Male and female.

Smith knelt before the drum. Its lid came unsealed at his touch--a wet pop! and a sucking sound. Into his naked lap poured a slew of squirming white bilge. Smith grinned. He ran his hands through the meaty-smelling muck, fascinated. Between his fingers wriggled the fresh white collops, the seed of the Father . . .

"It's still not too late, Daddy."

Yeah, sure, Smith thought. Of course!

The moonlight raged.

Jeannie nodded.

Smith put his face into the lumpen white slop, and began to eat.

Jeannie lay on the carpet before the tv, her chin in her little hands. *Star Trek* was her favorite show. Thank God Bones had put Spock's brain back in last night.

Upstairs, Smith thrilled. "I don't believe it."

"What, dear?"

"A black-throated blue warbler. Wow." Ah, well. He set down the binoculars and lay next to Donna in bed. It wouldn't be long now. She kissed him and smiled. Smith smiled too, and gently stroked the great gravid belly beneath the nightgown. It was bloated and lovely, stretched pin-prick tight, and so warm.

He put his ear to it and listened. He could *hear* them in there.

Donna fell asleep in his arms. Smith stroked the precious belly. He couldn't wait to see what came out.

The Wrong Guy

"We sure made a mess of him," Wendlyn remarked.

Rena cut a wicked grin. "Yeah. Neat, huh?"

Neither woman, by the way, wore panties. As they each leaned over the big opened trunk of the clay-red 76 Malibu, this fact would be obvious to any onlooker. Not that there would be any onlookers in proximity to the old Governor's Bridge at close to 4:30 in the morning. Nevertheless, the further over these two women leaned, the more of their backsides, i.e. rumps, i.e. glutius maximi, i.e. asses peeked out from beneath their shortish skirts. Rena wore tight blue leather. Wendlyn wore a more mature Ralph Lauren navy chino wrap.

"This one was fun," Rena said.

"Yeah," Wendlyn agreed. "A real scream, pun intended."

Rena giggled, "One less pretty-boy motherfucker to affront the society of women."

Moonlight dappled their well-lined backs and legs, wavering through high trees. An owl hooted. Below them, the gentle stream burbled over stones.

They both wore latex gloves as they tended to the corpse; just because they were impulsive didn't mean they were stupid. They'd read all about the state police carbon-dioxide lasers and special resin treatments that could lift fingerprints off human skin. No way these two gals were going to get caught. Wendlyn couldn't imagine anything more dreadful: doing life in the state slam, the dike wing. She was not adverse to the pleasures of a woman, but eating some 300-lb. cellblock mama's crusty cooze every night did not strike her as a pleasure. No, indeed.

"Shit!" Rena suddenly fretted. "Where's his—"

Wendlyn paused with the pliers, glaring. "God, you're so careless sometimes, Rena! You better find it! Did you leave it at the house?"

"Uh—" Rena blinked. "I don't think so."

"What about your purse? Did you put it in your purse?"

"Uuuuuuuuuuuh . . ."

"Rena, you should stand in front of a fan to change the air in your head! Honestly!"

"Well I'm sorry!" Rena whined, close to lacrimating. "I don't remember *what* I did with it!"

Wendlyn shook her head. *Kids,* she dismissed. *So unaware.* Rena was only 23, and quite flighty sometimes. Wendlyn, six years older, viewed her in a sense as a sister, that is at least when they weren't licking up each other's vaginal grooves. Sisters didn't generally partake in such practices. This was more an esoteric thing, a psychical/social bond, perhaps. They were sisters of the ether.

What had this one's name been? *Will?* Wendlyn thought. She'd never been good with names. *Walt.* There. That was it. They'd picked Walt up, without much effort, at Kaggies, one of the ruckus danceclubs downtown. Walt was one of those guys too good-looking for his own good. Rena and Wendlyn weren't too shabby themselves, mind you; they had the tackle to drag them in just as pretty as you please. Rena stood slim, trim, and alabaster-skinned, with short-cut shiny black hair. Wendlyn appeared more robust, a big, sturdy, curvaceous frame of plush flesh, with silken-straight white-blond hair, gem-blue eyes, and crisp tan lines. They rarely had trouble making a mark, and were always meticulously careful not to be seen leaving with a victim. Which might be worth pointing out now that not only were Wendlyn and Rena diverse, voracious, attractive, and highly sexualized women, they were also what psychiatrists would clinically label as systematized stage sociopaths with acute erotomanic impulses. Sex killers would be a less articulate label. Murderesses. Pure ass crazy psycho bitches . . .

Their philosophy was societal and rather militant in its feministic design. Never mind that they were fucked up in the head: abused, malnourished, and locked in closets as children, maladapted via unbridled drug and alcohol use and hence damaged of certain critical brain receptors, and, in general, rife with a plethora of environmentally-causated personality disorders and biogenic amine imbalances. They saw themselves instead as philosophers of the new dark age of sexual terror, chameleon siren songs of the nihilistic '90's. They did not perceive men, for instance, as individuals but as a cyclic and conspiratorial consortium bent on the total subjugation, exploitation, and sexual abuse of womanhood. They were pioneers of a sort, social guerrillas. Their manifesto was thus: since the beginning of civilization, man had freely and unconscionably exploited women. It was high time, therefore, that someone started exploiting them back.

Which led them, in their zeal, to some particularly brow-raising extremities. Walt, for example. Guilty by association. No doubt he'd exploited dozens, in not hundreds, of women with his looks and his phony charm. They'd taken him back to the house, for a "nightcap." Rena had his penis out before they even made it to the bedroom, her deft little hand exploring away on the burgeoning meat. That's all men were to them. Meat. They shared the remote little rancher Wendlyn's father had left her after his unfortunate "suicide" back in 88. He'd passed out drunk at his desk one night, after which Wendlyn had helped him along into the netherworld via a vintage Webley .455 revolver. Talk about a mess! And *loud?* Dad's brains looked like bloody chicken salad slopped across the fine lime and avocado print wallpaper. Anyway . . .

"Kinky babes, huh?" Walt had commented when Rena produced the four sets of handcuffs from the box under the bed. "You game?

They're just for atmosphere," she'd assured him. "Trick cuffs, see?" She put one on and demonstrated that a simple tug would release the locking ratchet. These cuffs in truth, however, were not trick cuffs at all but Peerless Model 26 police-issue detention cuffs, the Real McCoy, and what she *hadn't* shown the snide, cocky-smiling, and now fully erect Walt was the tiny shim she kept pressed against the ratchet during her demonstration. In other words, unbeknownst to Walt, once they got him stripped down and cuffed to the big brass bed, he was in there for the long haul.

Rena and Wendlyn stripped each other then, while Walt watched ga-ga-eyed from his low comfy vantage point. He looked quite silly now, handcuffed to a bed with his penis sticking up like a pulsing, tumescent root. "Yeah, this is hell, ain't it?" Walt joked next when his two suitors commenced with the tongue bath. "Yeah, some tough life, I'll tell ya." *Shut up, Walt,* Wendlyn felt like saying, alternately licking his testicles. Rena gave Walt's mouth something to do besides jabber, inserting a nipple into it and instructing, "Suck, Walt. Just keep quiet and suck." Walt sucked, with no reservations. Rena's breasts, i.e. hooters, i.e. rib melons, i.e. tits, were smallish yet quite interesting: pointed, with bounce, and ornamented by big distended brownish cones, while Wendlyn proved more conventional in regards to the mystic thing known as the human mammarian carriage—a formidable rack of firm buoyant 38D's with large pink areolae and nipple ends akin to thimbles. An equal distinction existed, respective of the manner in which they maintained the outer geographies of their sexual real estate. Rena had spent serious money electrolocizing the entirety of her pubis, while Wendlyn preferred a more unruly state of affairs, displaying a big, dense, extruding light-blond bush.

And it was into this same bush that, next, the shaft of Walt's sexual architecture eagerly disappeared. Wendlyn very articulately responded "Oooooooo," to this gesture, as Rena masturbated to the frictive and delicious sensation of having her coney nipples sucked.

Wendlyn rode him awhile, then queried, "Ready, Rena?"

Out popped the nipple from Walt's lips. "Yeah," she said.

"Ready for what?" Walt breathily inquired as Wendlyn's gorgeous broad bottom continued to rise and plunge. It was her own curiosity that founded this latest escapade. During a short stint as a nursing assistant, she'd read in the *American Journal of Psychiatry* an article about sexual response during that ever rare occasion of Female-to-Male Rape. This article claimed that, when threatened by death or grievous injury, the human body would respond to any demand that might increase the likelihood of survival. In other words, for instance, if a man with a gun to his head was told to fuck, by golly, those libidinal hormones would make damn sure he was able to, maintaining an erection in spite of the undeniably non-arousing circumstances.

Only it was not a gun that Rena produced from the macabre toy box under the bed.

It was a pair of tin snips.

"Holy fucking shit!" Walt yelled, as would most any man in this same predicament.

"Quiet, Walt. And listen." Wendlyn eased all the way down on Walt's cock, adroitly flexing her vaginal muscles as she explained the details of this latest sociopathic supposition. "It's this simple. I'm going to fuck you, and if you go soft on me, Rena here will cut off your cock with those tin snips. Is that perfectly clear?"

About the only thing *perfectly* clear to Walt just then was that he was in some shit of monumental depth. He responded quite stupidly, as men often do, by avoiding the question. He jerked his wrists against the cuffs and with great befuddlement exclaimed: "These aren't trick cuffs!"

"No, Walt, they're not," Rena replied, displaying the hard-steel heavy-gauge snips. "And it doesn't look to me like there's a whole hell of a lot you can do about that."

snip-snip, whispered the tin snips in the air.

Wendlyn, with lewd grin and narrowed eyes, soon found that the

American Journal of Psychiatry was quite accurate in their claim. Walt's cock, despite this freight of human terror, did not surrender one iota of its spongal turgidity. If anything, it grew even more stiff within the damp, excited confines of Wendlyn's reproductive channel, i.e. vaginal pass, i.e. birth canal, i.e. pussy. Rena, meanwhile, opened and closed the tin snips before Walt's bulging eyeballs, explicating, "We're killers, Walt"—*snip-snip-snip*—"we're psycho-sexual *killers*"—*snip-snip-snip*—"and we've murdered over a dozen men in the last year." *snip-snip-snip.* "I'll bet that makes your cock just want to go limp as an overcooked noodle, hmmm?"

Walt's cock did no such thing, remaining stiff as a polished nightstick. Wendlyn leaned forward in her greedy straddle, accelerating the pace of the congress until her flexing, well-lubricated loins gave way in luscious throbbing thrumming orgasm . . .

"There," Rena consoled, smiling down between her unique, elongated breasts. She patted his tummy.

Wendlyn climbed off. "You did it, Walt. You're a standup guy."

"Yuh-yuh-you're gonna let me go now, right?" Walt asked.

"Nuh-nuh-no, Walt," Rena answered. "We're going to cut your cock off."

Walt was quite understandably outraged by this bit of information, and he began to snap his ankles and wrists madly, and quite uselessly, against their stainless steel fetters, blubbering: "Buh-buh-but you said if I didn't guh-guh-go soft, yuh-yuh-you wouldn't—"

"Don't be a doe-doe, Walt," Rena suggested, delighted by his state of prostrate and inescapable horror. "Don't be *stupid.*"

Wendlyn's pretty face grew alight in the knowing grin. "We just got done telling you that we're killers, and if we're killers, it only stands to reason that we're probably liars, too."

The tin snips slowly opened, like jaws.

Walt began to scream, as Rena began to snip.

Which left them now in their current quandary, at precisely 4:26 in the morning, parked on the old Governor's Bridge. Rena desperately rummaged through the Malibu's cargo-hold-sized trunk. Where was it? Where was Walt's dick?

Rena started crying.

"Oh, now," Wendlyn tried to soothe her, rubbing her back. "Don't worry about it. It's not like he can be identified by his *cock.*"

This was true, unless of course the police had some secret new system of genital identification. Wendlyn smiled to herself. Perhaps one day she'd open the fridge and see a picture of Walt's *dick* printed on a milk carton. There were, however, some other things that Walt definitely *could be* identified by, thirty-two of which Wendlyn now went to considerable effort to take care of. Before the nursing job, she'd been a dental technician, but that didn't make the task of extracting Walt's teeth any less laborious. The pliers were difficult to manipulate in such limited oral space. Eventually, though, she managed to get them all out of Walt's dead maw, whereupon she placed them all into a small cloth sack.

Rena was still crying, rummaging. She was checking the tool box, for God's sake, and the plastic cooler they used when they went to the beach. "Oh, Wendy, I'm sorry! Where could it be? Did I leave it on the dresser with the keys? The kitchen counter?"

"Rena, I told you. Forget about his cock. Here. Help me get him out."

They travailed then to lifting out the plastic dropcloth in which the deader-than-dogshit Walt had been carefully becloaked. Rena hammered the little bag of teeth against the asphalt with a four-pound sledge, until all were sufficiently pulverized. Wendlyn, meanwhile, removed the glass flask (one of many perks of working in a hospital) and emptied its teeming contents onto Walt's remaining identifiable features. The concentrated nitric acid made short work of the hands and feet, fizzing away any and all ridge prints, loops, whorls, and bifurcations. Walt's face, too, bubbled away with equal steaming vigor.

The unappreciated separation of his genitals from his groin, by the way, had not of itself spelled Walt's demise. He'd screamed loud and hard as a horn on a semi-rig, thrashing amid his Peerless-handcuff trap, but had surprisingly not died. Nor had Wendlyn's delvings with the Clay Adams brand bivalving scalpel done the trick. It got quite ugly, Walt screaming like that, and thrashing away with no penis. Blood gushed like Great Falls. Eventually Rena had stuck a knitting needle up his nose, driving it back with her palm deep into the meat of Walt's parietal lobe. She'd jiggled it around a few times, until he checked out.

"Ashame about his face," Rena lamented now, looking down in the moonlight. "He could've been on the cover of *GQ.*"

"Not anymore. *Fangoria,* maybe. Say goodnight, Walt."

They hefted up either end of the dropcloth and rolled it over the rusty metal bridge rail. *Ka-SPLASH!* The moonlight rippled spectacularly.

Then they were driving away, off into the warm, star-chipped night. "Wendy, look!" Rena celebrated, bending over in the passenger seat. "I found Walt's dick!"

So she had; somehow, Walt's severed member had found its way to the footwell. "Now I remember. I brought it along to diddle with while we were driving out." Rena picked it up and, ever the comedian, slid back her blue-leather skirt and held Walt's now seriously shriveled cock to her clitoris, spreading her trim legs. "Look, Wendy! I've got a penis! I'm a man!"

Wendlyn rolled her eyes behind the wheel. "You're so silly sometimes. Honestly." She took the wizened thing and flipped it out the window, where eventually it would be eaten by possums.

Wendlyn expertly plunged the dual Doc Johnson vibrators in and out of Rena's off-pink vulva and rectum, licking the swollen clitoris. Rena squirmed, sighing through her grin, as Claudius, the largest of her three pet hognose snakes, slithered about her belly and pointed breasts. Rena was possessed of some rather left-field eccentricities, several of which Wendlyn was hard-pressed to tolerate: Heineken douches, Bull Frog Stuffing, electric ben-wa balls up her ass whilst in public. Plus snakes. They'd met at North County General, where Rena was a floor receptionist. Wendlyn, a Class I nurses' aide, caught Rena masturbating in the janitorial closet one night, with a polypropylene Bacti-Capall culture tube and hemostats clipped to her nipples. "Ooops," Rena had said. Instead of filling out an employee negligence report, Wendlyn had sealed their friendship by immediately planting her big blond pubis in Rena's face. Their careers, though, had ended rather expeditiously. Rena had been fired for stealing an array of controlled pharmaceuticals from the nurses' station, while Wendlyn, shortly thereafter, had received her walking papers for "gross sexual misconduct upon the hospital premise." A staff doctor had pulled back a privacy curtain in an end ICU cove, to discover the ever-curious Wendlyn fastidiously fellating a male critical coma patient. "I wanted to see if a brain-dead person could come," she'd explained. "You're fired," the doctor had replied.

Oh, well. Nevertheless, their friendship remained, and to make a long exposition short, they soon found a vivid compatibility in their ravenous sexualities as well as their sociopathies. In no time at all, they were murdering men at about a rate of one a month, through all manner of demented imagination: gastric lavage with Clorox, non-anesthetic live dissection, brain surgery with power tools, and acts of genital mayhem that copuld only be described as "bigtime." Once they'd catheterized a bartender and filled his bladder with 5W 30-grade motor oil, then ice-picked his lower abdomen to watch the oil ooze out. Another time Wendlyn was blowing some dolt they'd picked up at the races; Rena had clipped off his testicles at the precise moment of his climax. Once they'd even dissected a penis, on a living "patient," removing all the skin and the entire scrotum, after which Rena had clipped off the raw shaft a quarter inch at a time. This guy had screamed so loud they'd had to put cotton in their ears! One pickup had gotten rude with them, actually hailing such invectives as: "Bitches! Lesbos! Psychopaths!" Wendlyn had opened his anus with a pair of rectal retractors stolen from the hospital, while Rena, with more than a smidgen of difficulty, had inserted Tiberius, one of her pet hognose snakes, into the offender's bowel. Tiberius had churned away for quite some time in there, before finally giving up the ghost, while their unmannerly companion had screamed shock-eyed and blue in the face. "Poor Tiberius," Rena regretted. She'd finished the man off by carefully drilling a shallow hole in his skull with a 1/4-inch carbon bit, then slowly inserting long carpet needles and autopsy pins into the hole. Genital electrocution, ground-glass and/or boiling bacon grease enemas, ice picks in the ears and/or eyes, Coca-Cola blood transfusions, total body flensing, and, of course, what Rena referred to as "dick-scarfing." Nothing would get a fella screaming faster and louder than having his pride and joy and family jewels nimbly chewed off by a pair of crazier-than-shithouse-rats militant feminists. No, sir. You name it, Wendlyn and Rena did it, much to the disconsolation of many a man, and all in the name of their righteous ideology, to vindicate roughly seventy centuries of subjugation.

Plus, it was fun, at least from the standpoint of a clinical sociopath

One thing they never considered, though, was the possibility that sooner or later they might pick the wrong guy . . .

Larry seemed a little fat and doty; pickings were slim some nights. He provided at least the necessary prerequisites: your typical gaping, gawping, lustful cockhound/ nutchase/Feel-'Um-Fuck 'Um-And-Forget-'Um Man. At the bar, Larry's eyes had been all over them, and eventually so had his hands. He'd plied them with drinks and smothered them with overtly suggestive remarks, foremost of which was: "What say we get outa this gin joint? I could show you two babes a really hot time." He'd actually winked then, and gave Rena's little rump a pat. Wendlyn smirked. *A hot time?* she thought. *We'll see who shows who a hot time.* She got wet just thinking about it.

Back at the house, Larry had offered no protestations whatsoever to Rena's "trick" cuffs. "I'm easy," he'd chuckled as they'd cuffed him down. Naked, he looked like dough stretched out on the bed, beer gut, no muscles, but . . . *Hmmm,* Wendlyn considered, appraising his works, which, despite their flaccidity, looked very promising. Rena sat at once on his face, her sleek back to the wall, as Wendlyn perked him up with her hand. "Jesus Christ!" Rena delighted. "You're gonna need a shoe horn to sit on all of that!" *You ain't kidding,* Wendlyn thought, plying the hardening tube of flesh. Larry's genitals bloomed; Wendlyn smiled giddily. "This looks like something that should hang in a smokehouse." Larry easily sported a twelve-inch root, with the girth of a pony bottle. Wendlyn reveled in its shape, its colossal well-formed glans, fat veins, and a urethral ingress big enough to admit her pinkie. Even his testicles were monsters: heavy and hot, and large as Jumbo Grade-A eggs. Wendlyn wasted no time in mounting this wonderful gorged pole, which actually nudged the cap of her cervix each time she rode down. She and Rena faced each other now, both murmuring and rolling their eyes at Larry's oral and copulatory prowess.

"His tongue must be as big as his cock," Rena was very happy to relate, gritting her teeth through a lascivious grin. "Feels like it's going right up my fuckin' uterus!"

"He can fuck too," Wendlyn assured, grinning much the same. This was so good—so slow and luscious and *hot*; she was actually drooling. *Fucking, my foot,* she thought. *This isn't fucking, it's deep-well drilling, and Larry Boy's about to tap the pool.*

Indeed, Larry's penis felt more akin to one of those extra-long tubes of chocolate-chip cookie dough; this thing was squeezing her g-spot her flat against her anterior wall. Shit, she didn't even know she *had* a g-spot until now. Wendlyn's reproductive orifice was no stranger to phalli of above-average proportions, but this—*this*—was ridiculous! That Miller Pony-Bottle girth stretched her vulva out to a tight delicious bright-pink rim, plowing steadfast as a derrick wheel, while the length continued to plumb the absolute extremities of the tract of her womanhood. She felt skewered: Wendlyn-ka-bob. Quaking multiple orgasms went off deep in her loins like subsurface demolition. Her vagina pulsed and pulsed, wringing pleasure out of her nerves much the same as a hand wringing milk out of a cow's gorged teat. Exhausted, then, she switched positions with Rena, who immediately exclaimed "It's like fucking a rolling pin, Wendy!" as she inserted the elephantine penis into her slick bald snatch. Wendlyn found no exaggeration in Rena's previous affirmation; when she pressed her own downy-blond snatch to Larry's face, a tongue of utmost dimensions delved at once up into the beslickened furrow. She came again in minutes, leaving Larry's face shiny as wet shellack, and then Rena, too, tensed up and shuddered in wave upon wave of deepest orgasm, at which time Larry's own crisis unloosed, warm gouts of semen fat as worms rocketing up into the squirming purse of flesh. Rena's face strained, her hands opened on his belly, as she squealed in glee, "He's coming in me like a fucking garden hose!"

"Whew!" Larry replied, laxing back against the handcuffs. "That was one dandy nut. I knew you girls were hot."

"And we're gonna get a lot hotter," Wendlyn promised. Larry didn't notice Rena leaving the room, too engrossed via the next distraction: the application of Wendlyn's mouth to the flaccid, veined penis. It didn't remain flaccid long, though. In only minutes, back to turgid life it sprang. Wendlyn 69'd him, already anxious to feel that long tongue slide back up into her groove's salt-wet depths. To her surprise, however, and in an ultimate display of male bravado, the tongue bypassed this usual fissure and forced its way instead into the tight, flinching button of her rectum. It took quite a man to offer his tongue to this less-dainty orifice and, likewise, it took quite a woman to sufficiently perform fellatio upon a cock like Larry's. She could scarcely get the glans in her mouth much less the tumid shaft—she'd have better luck sucking a summer squash! Eventually she took to drawing her pinkie in and out of the big peehole, the sensation of which Larry tittered at as his visage remained vised in the cleft of Wendlyn's buttocks.

But when Rena reappeared, she climbed off. "You said you wanted a hot time, right, Larry?"

"Oh, yeah, oh, yeah," Larry concurred. His penis bobbed, like a ludicrous puppet.

"Well how's this for hot?" Rena stepped into the light, wearing sunglasses, for a reason that would become apparent in another moment. In her left hand she held a match. And in her right hand she held--

"OH, MY GOD!" Larry justifiably screamed.

—a blowtorch.

"This should be *real* hot, Larry," Wendlyn proposed. She pressed her breasts together in sheer, erotic delight. "And I mean *real real* hot . . ."

Rena lit the blowtorch and adjusted its flame down to a hissing, white-blue point. "Hot enough for you, Larry?" she inquired, applying the 1200-degree-plus flame to the tip of his dick. The tip shriveled at once, like a smoking marshmallow. Ditto as for the big testicles. Rena languidly roved the torch flame back and forth across the crisping scrotum, while Larry screamed so hard the whites of his eyes turned red in hemorrhage, and thrashed with such force the bed rocked up and down on its legs.

Wendlyn waved away at the stinking smoke, laughing along like a naked blond cheerleader from hell. Rena next bore the flame down on the center of Larry's flabby chest, straddling him as he bucked horselike in agony better left undescribed. The flame burned down down down, disintegrating flesh and bone alike, opening up a great black smoking pit in which Larry's heart cooked, then broiled, then collapsed to ash.

So much for Larry.

"Yeah," Wendlyn remarked, grinning down through the

odiferous smoke. "I think that was hot enough for him."

Wendlyn sauntered nude to the garage, to fetch a dropcloth.

Her big orbicular breasts bounced quite nicely with each step, and her big smile made no secret of her satisfaction. *Chalk up another one for womanhood,* she thought. *One more greedy, lustful, pussy-hungry woman-exploiter for the deep six.*

Back in the bedroom, though, she froze.

"What the . . . *fuck?*"

The bed lay empty. At first she thought Rena must already have unlocked the corpse, but a closer glance invalidated this suspicion. Each set of handcuffs remained secured to the bed's brass rails, yet each set was clearly missing its counterpart. In other words, the cuffs had been broken . . .

And above the lingering smoky stench of fried human flesh, Wendlyn smelled something deeper, more pungent. Like fresh sewage enlaced with something else . . .

Then she glanced to the left—

Glanced down—

And screamed.

Out of the room's shadow, Rena lay sprawled in the corner, glassy-eyed in death. Some heinously sharp instrument had lain open her abdomen, and from this gaping insult most of her lower g.i. tract had been yanked out. Shiny pink intestines formed squiggles on the floor, like queer garlands. Kidneys, spleen, and pancreas glistened. Worse, though, was that Rena's adorable, pointy little breasts were... gone. Bitten off. And the same too for that silk-smooth hairless pubis: gnawed out from betwixt the askew legs.

Beady eyes glinted. From the shadow, the huge angular head lowered as similarly huge jaws spread, baring white teeth the size of masonry nails. Rena's face was then eaten off the skull as a child might eat the icing off a cupcake.

A cascade of warm amber pee flowed freely down Wendlyn's

plush legs. Her mouth froze open. She couldn't move. Then the voice croaked, but it was no human voice at all—just a ragged, unearthly suboctave, a succession of rasps, rattling like phlegm.

The voice said this: "You picked the wrong guy to fuck with tonight, baby."

By now Larry had transformed to near completeness, and this ancient and mystical metamorphosis had fully repaired Rena's earlier handiwork with the blowtorch. Three lone facts stood before Wendlyn now which, despite their impossibility, she could not deny. One, Larry was alive. Two, he was pissed off. And, three, he was a werewolf.

Wendlyn gulped.

Correction. He was a *big* werewolf, and in more ways than one. No reckoning would save her now, nor would any defensive action, and certainly no plea. Despite her understandable horror, however, and the paresis from which she could not release herself, the cogent agreement sparkled in her mind. *Yes. Yes, you're right. We definitely picked the wrong guy to fuck with tonight.*

So much for counter-exploitation.

The creature rose, the vulpine face grinned. Well-hung as a man, Larry was even bigger as a lycantrope, the evidence of which now bloomed in obviousness, the doglike sheath sliding back showing glinting, shiny pink. Poor Wendlyn easily acknowledged the deduction: Now that Larry had eaten, he was ready to get down to some serious exploitation of his own.

The Baby

Rosser kind of joggled on the bus, rocking in his seat. It was a county bus, he presumed, Russell County, one of the poorest, so it made sense that the coach lacked air-conditioning. He felt like he was cooking in his jeans, his soiled Christian Dior shirt adhered to him by sweat, his feet baking in K-Mart sneakers. He'd only lived in Luntville a week, chased here, he guessed, by either penance or bad karma. The heat seemed to be chasing him too. The bus rocked and rocked.

Maybe I'm actually in hell, he considered. *Hell can't possibly be any hotter than this.* Nor its population any uglier. The bus driver looked like Lurch. The big guy in overalls in back looked like Shrek, and the woman sitting across could easily have been a female version of Don King.

Everything beyond the window appeared as desolate as his thoughts. *Fall guy, Patsy—call it what you want. I got screwed and I can't unscrew myself.* Rosser was a project manager for a major construction company—er, had been. Now he was a fleeing felon. Ordinarily he might get a year or two in jail and be out on good behavior after a few months, when illegal cost-cutting lead to deaths. But *this?* It had been Barren and Franks, company's owners, who'd charged the client for the firewalls they hadn't really installed. Same with the extra load-bearing beams in the center of the complex. The client paid for it—they had to, via state building codes—but Barren and Franks had "forgotten" to include these items in the

126

actual construction of the site—and pocketed the money. Hence, little more than a week after the day-care center had opened, a roof strut had collapsed, severing a gas line, and the center had exploded like something carpet-bombed. Three dozen toddlers burned up like bacon, not to mention a number of adults. Barren and Franks had greased the right palms, forged the right invoices and deposit receipts, and bribed some "eyewitnesses," and that was that.

Business degree from Georgetown, minor in architecture. A brand-new Audi, and $150,000-a-year salary. All gone. All up in smoke. *I'm not up Shit's Creek without a paddle,* he thought. *I'm in the middle of the Shit Sea without a boat.*

Rosser beat the warrant-issuing deputy sheriffs by a half hour, went to the company office, cleaned out the safe, and hitchhiked out of town. He kept hitching till he was halfway across the county, then Greyhounded here, here being Luntville, in southern Virginia, which made the little burg in *Green Acres* look like Harvard Yard. *God Almighty,* he'd thought when he first arrived. It was another world, a secret world within the Land of Opportunity. Generations of families who didn't know what education was. Mind-boggling poverty. Unemployment. Desperation, adultery, and alcoholism as the status quo.

A man sitting next to Rosser grinned at him in a way that seemed knowing. The grin was black. Teeth like pegs of licorice. The guy had greased-stained jeans and a similarly stained gas-station shirt with the name tag COREY. Shoulder-length stringy hair hung down from the grime-edged REMINGTON baseball hat. He just kept grinning, right at Rosser.

Is this the guy from Deliverance? Rosser flinched, tried not to meet his eyes. Why was the man staring?

"You runnin'?"

"Pardon me?" Rosser asked.

"Never mind." Corey pronounced "mind" as "mand." "I was, awhile's back. Couldn't hack it no more. Wife got fat, baby whined all night like a bad water pump. One day I'se blinked and thunk *what the fuck did you git yer 'self into, you moe-ron?* So I split. Couldn't stay in Stone Gap. Shee-it, wife's family lived there–if I'd even started *talkin'* 'bout divorce'n shit, her fucked-up kin'd come after me with pitchforks'n shovels." The rotten grin, somehow, brightened. "The fuckin' was good, though. At least good enough to knock the pig up."

Invigorating conversation, Rosser thought.

The bus banged over a pothole. "Anyways, that's how I'se landed here." The grin, more of the grin. "Just like you, I suppose. Am I right?"

"Not altogether," Rosser admitted. "What makes you think I'm . . . running?"

A phlegmy chuckle. "Come on. That white button-down shirt? Looks like a business shirt that you're just wearing cos it's all ya got. Ain't no businessmen in these parts. Ain't no business."

Suddenly Rosser felt foolish in the office shirt, a sore thumb. "You could say I recently elected to relocate . . ." He didn't want to talk at all, but the question came unbidden, irresistibly: "How-how long ago was this?"

The grin jolted forward. "Was *what?*"

"How long ago did you leave your wife and child? Er, I mean, how long have you been here, in this area?"

"Six, seven years thereabouts."

Sounded promising, at least. If this redneck grease monkey started a new life in Luntville, so could Rosser. Who would look for him here? The beard was already growing in, the hair lengthening, dyed dirty-blond. The couple hundred grand he'd taken out of the safe could go a long, long time in an economy like this. He'd get some under the table job somewhere, become part of the scenery— and part of a town and population that no one gave a shit about. This was his chance.

And better than Corey's, right? Rosser had left no wife and child behind, and he had some smarts and an education that would covertly come in handy, so long as he laid low. *Things could be worse,* he realized.

Optimism couldn't hurt.

"So you're—what?—a mechanic?" Rosser inquired next.

Corey stunk like a cross between a Jiffy Lube and an armpit. "Shore, down at Hull's garage next to the general store," the black grin answered. "I just do my job, get my paycheck, mind my own business. Works out just fine, ya know?"

Just another example of what Rosser needed reinforced. A person *could* start a new life, an *anonymous* life, and leave the past behind. Certainly Rosser hoped he never saw Corey and his rotten grin ever again, but he did appreciate the confidence of his example. The past was the past. Fate had given him a new future, and Rosser was determined to make the best of it.

The shit-hole rooming house he lived in was miles from the nearest store; hence, the bus ride. Store-brand tortilla chips and a can of spaghetti would be dinner. And at the dollar store he'd picked up several cheap t-shirts and pairs of socks. He was serious about this. Thus far it seemed that the landlady approved of him: Mrs. Doberman (that's right, *Doberman,* and her name suited her). "A fine, fine young man," she'd commented this morning when he'd left. "So intelligent and polite . . . and so handsome!" He'd get a radio soon, a TV, gradually accrue the barest necessities. The more he thought about it, the better he felt.

"Check it out, Hoss," Corey said. At the next stop off State Route 154, a heavyset woman clodded on, grocery bag under one arm, a baby under the other. She turned around, clumsily manipulating herself, as though preparing to sit down required some urgent consideration. Corey further remarked, "Jesus Christ, is it gonna take all fuckin' day for her to sit her fat ass down?" Eventually, the woman sat down in the bench seat right behind Lurch, and the bus . . . lurched on.

White Trash Nation, Rosser mused, eyeing her. Did the woman smile at him? *I hope not. She smiled at Corey,* he convinced himself. The woman was hideous. Broken teeth, crooked nose, frizzed hair the color of dirty dishwater. The baby hung off her left side; he couldn't really see it save for a pudgy, dirty leg sticking out across the area of space that ordinarily would've been called a lap. Wet, glurpy noises could be heard, however: baby sounds. Peeking from the top of the grocery bag were Twinkies, donuts, a six-pack of Keystone.

Rosser wasn't sure what Corey whispered under his breath, but he thought it was: "I'm so horny I could spit on the floor and hump the spit."

Her bloodshot eyes darted quickly to him again, then quickly away: a White Trash flirt. *No, no, the glance was to Corey, to Corey.*

Corey slapped him on the back. "Looks like this is your lucky day, huh, Hoss? Shit if she ain't got the hots for ya."

"Not for me, for you. Either that or she knows you."

"Oh, I know the look." An elbow jab. "But do me a favor. Lemme have some sloppy seconds, will ya? Shee-it, bet she'd do us both fer free on account she's hot for you. Her name's Maxine, by the way."

"So you *do* know her," Rosser said.

"Any horny fella with an extra sawbuck knows her. She's the bottom of the barrel pussy in Luntville. Just plop the fat bitch down on the floor, spread those legs, spit on that pie, hold yer nose, and stick it in. Hump it hard, hump it fast, and fill her up. A nut's a nut, ya know? And she don't make ya use none of that condom shit." Another comradely slap to the back. "Not a bad lay if ya keep yer eyes closed and don't breathe." Corey laughed loud enough to turn several heads, just not Maxine's.

So. The local prostitute, Rosser assessed. More of the social dynamic, however pitiful. Rosser could not fathom the man desperate enough to have sexual congress with this human beast. Her face looked puffed, shiny in sunburn. Moles like raisins studded the roll of fat around her neck. Indeed, here was definitive white trash.

Four-foot-eleven in her flip-flops, and an easy one-seventy on the scale. The enormous breasts looked flattened in the bland sundress, laying atop a distended junk-food belly. Cellulite-runneled legs wide as fifty-pound sacks of rice, with skin the color of, well . . . rice. Her hair could've been a floor mop stained pitch-black. The outlines of lopsided nipples the size of beer coasters ghosted through the top's shabby fabric.

He still couldn't see any details of the baby.

"Get a load of the belly on her, huh?" came Corey's next enlightening observation. "Gotta wonder if she's knocked up again. Ya never can tell with some of these girls." Corey openly rubbed his crotch. "A'course, if she ain't, I'd be more'n happy ta fuck up her life a little more'n put another white-trash food-stamp bun in her fat cracker oven."

Rosser wilted.

"Next stop, Crick City crossroads," the driver announced. "Connection for the Number Three bus."

Somebody rang the bell and the bus shimmied to a stop. A teenager sitting behind Shrek moved forward for the doors, but Rosser was looking outside at the bus shelter. In the shelter stood at startlingly attractive woman in her mid-twenties. Shimmering blond hair, cut-off jeans and a blazing white halter. Nut-brown tan and legs that never ended. Rosser gulped at the vision, his most spontaneous lust ignited at once. *Please, please,* he pleaded. *Please get on the bus.* Not that he would do anything, make conversation, make a move— nothing like that. Rosser knew well that he'd never stand a chance with such a local. He merely hoped she'd get on the bus so he could look at her, just to see something lovely.

But she made no gesture to get on.

"How'd ya like to park a wad up *that* twat, Hoss?" Corey tittered. "I'd hump her from one end of the floor to the other. Pop the first one in her cut, then jerk off another in her face. Cream the bitch up fierce, huh, Hoss?"

131

In spite of the appallingly vulgar words, the image was irresistible, and just as Rosser noticed the lusty spark in his penis, his partner said, "Shee-it, practically got me full wood just *lookin'* at that. How 'bout you, Hoss?" A chuckle through the black grin. "Think ya just might be able to git it up fer a piece'a that angel-food-cake pussy?"

Rosser's erection flexed, straining against the confines of his shorts. "I'd say the prospect of that circumstance presents a very *high* order of probability."

Corey cracked out a guffaw and clapped his hands. "Stranger, I don't know *what* the fuck you just said but I shore like the way you talk!"

No, the blonde wasn't getting on but the passenger was now getting off. The scruffy kid didn't even look twenty: long hair, baggy shorts, sneakers with no laces, no shirt.

"Damn boy must be et up with a case of the dumb-ass," Corey remarked.

"What?"

"The punk's Jess Fuller. Been run out'a town twice and now he's back."

"What was he run out of town for?"

"Makes that crystal-meth shit in his trailer, sells it ta kids."

"What about the police? He should be in jail."

"Cops down here ain't got time, they'se all on the take for the moonshiners up in the hills. They get a cut for every run they protect into Kentucky. The 'shiners make it here, sell ta the dry counties across the line."

An interesting societal commentary, at the very least. Rosser was uncomfortable but, at the same time, fascinated. *No. I am definitely not from around here.*

As the punk debarked, Rosser's eyes flicked back to the window, to the blonde. Seeing her seemed akin to a man in the desert stumbling into an oasis. Sweat glimmered in her cleavage. His eyes ran up her legs to the flat, impeccably tanned abdomen, the petite slit for a navel. *Jesus wept.* The waist of her cut-offs seemed to draw a line just above where her pubic hair would start, and the seam between her legs divided her vulva through the faded denim. Rosser sighed.

Then noticed something.

The blonde seemed alarmed; she was stepping back. Two tall bulky figures came around the stand of trees at one side of the bus shelter. Two more identical figures came around from the other side.

What's this?

"Looks like the jig is up fer Fuller," Corey said.

Outside, a confrontation began. The four tall bulky figures were indeed identical, brawny boys in their late teens, identical buzzcuts, identical shorts and shirts. Identical faces.

"Christ, they're—" Rosser began.

"The Harkins boys. Quadruplets. They're all nineteen er thereabouts. And lemme tell ya, they don't take no shit. As bad-ass a crew as you'll ever wanna meet. Watch."

Rosser watched, all right. The quadruplets surrounded the punk named Fuller. There was some laughing, shoving, while Fuller pleaded the likes of: "I ain't done nothin' to you guys! I ain't sellin' ice no more, I swear!" and on and on, but the Harkins boys wouldn't hear of it.

"Looks like we're about to see a good old fashioned ass-kicking," Rosser observed.

"Oh, it'll be a tad more'n that, Hoss."

One of the quadruplets', in a split-second, slammed a knuckly fist to Fuller's head. Rosser's teeth ground—the blow sounded like wet leather snapping—and that was all for Fuller. He was out cold, flat on his back.

Next, the boys were pulling off Fuller's baggy shorts.

What in God's name? Rosser thought.

"Bet they do a mallet-job on him," Corey guessed.

"What?"

"Fuck his balls all up is what. Look–see? The one on the end . . ."

Rosser's eyes darted to the last boy, who was hefting a large hubcap mallet while the others cackled.

"Come on, Tucker! Let 'er rip!"

"Teach this cracker piece'a shit not to sell drugs in our town—"

"Sells it ta kids, fer shit's sake."

"Do it! Do it!"

The quadruplet named Tucker knelt down, while another boy held Fuller's shriveled penis back so that it wasn't laying over the scrotum. Then—

WHAP! WHAP! WHAP!

Over and over again, Tucker smacked the scrotum with the mallet. Each blow caused Fuller to shudder in spite of unconsciousness.

WHAP! WHAP! WHAP!

Over and over.

Rosser was grateful that he couldn't see the details.

"Shee-it, Hoss. Ain't no nuts left in that sack, you can count on it. They'se mush. They done popped his balls."

Rosser didn't need the elaboration. He rushed up to the driver, who'd kept to door open so he could watch the foray. "You must have a radio or something on this bus," Rosser demanded. "Call the police!"

Lurch looked blankly at him. "Why?"

"*Why?* There's a major assault going on out there!"

"Ain't no need fer police. Things down here have a way of takin' care of themselves. When somethin' ain't right, the Harkins boys fix it."

Rosser felt uselessly outraged.

"Sit back down, Hoss." Corey was pulling him back to his seat. "This is how things work down here is all. You'll git used to it. Besides, you're missin' the show!"

Rosser sat back down, dazed. He couldn't believe this. Corey continued to talk but only half the words were getting through: "—back shore is a motherfucker, huh?" and "—teach his ass." Then:

134

"Look, now they're gonna dick-snaggle him."

Something roused Rosser from the outrage. "What did you say?"

"Ain't never heard of a dick-snagglin'? Shee-it, Hoss. Watch. Learn somethin'."

Rosser dared to let his gaze return to the window. One of the quadruplets was now gnawing on Fuller's penis.

Not biting it off. Just gnawing, as if on a tough piece of steak.

Rosser's stomach churned churning.

Lurch grinned back at Corey, tittering. "Ain't seen me a good dick-snagglin' in a long spell."

"Me neithers! It's a sight, ain't it?"

"That it is . . ."

The festivities outside were coming to an end. The blonde stood at the other end of the shelter, smoking. She didn't seem at all concerned. *An everyday occurrence?* Rosser wondered absurdly. *Dick-snaggling? My God.*

"Well," one of the Harkins said, "if he don't learn this time, he ain't never gonna learn."

"Oh, and just so ya cain't make no more crystal—"

WHAP! WHAP!

One of the Harkins smashed each of Fuller's hands with the mallet. The punk heaved, convulsing.

"Break his legs, too!"

"Naw, ya dope. He cain't leave town with busted legs."

"He ever comes back? We'll just kill the piece of shit'n be done with it."

"We should'a done that this time."

"Yeah, but this is more fun."

More fun, Rosser thought.

The Harkin's boys disbanded. The blonde tapped an ash. Did she wink at Rosser? He was too disarrayed to even think about it, and after the atrocity he'd just witnessed, sex was far from his mind.

But not Corey's, evidently. "Yeah, I'd punch blondie's little hole but good. Bet she squeaks when ya fuck her, huh? Then I'd flip her over fer a butt-fuckin'. Man, I'd come so much up her ass, she'd shit cream fer a week."

Rosser felt nauseous. The day was dead for him, and it was only afternoon. Indeed, he needed to come to a different world and, by God, he'd found it.

The driver snapped the door shut and put the bus in gear. Before he pulled away from the stop, Corey looked right at the blonde and licked his lips.

"Corey Ryan, what'choo lookin' out there at that skinny bitch for?" the woman with the baby said in an irritatingly high drawl. She crudely hefted a breast in her hand. "You wanna real woman, you know where she is."

Corey promptly responded, "I'll tell ya where she *ain't*, Maxine. On this bus."

But the woman just smiled coyly at the insult. "Oh, you know you want it. You cain't jive me."

Corey leaned to one side and cut a fart.

Oh, man, Rosser thought. *I am so out of my element.*

The monotonous scenery rolled by in the window. Rosser's thoughts blanked. More glurpy baby noises resounded, and Corey was rubbing his crotch.

"Next stop, Pegleg Road, connection to Luntville crossroads," the driver announced. Rosser wearily raised his hand to pull the bell but it rang before he could. When he looked over, he saw the fat woman lowering her arm.

Corey chuckled gutturally. "Looks like she'n you're gettin' off the same stop. Have fun. Drop some wax fer me, will ya?"

Rosser shook his head.

"Look, I know what'cher thinkin'."

"What am I thinking, Corey? Please. Tell me."

"You're thinkin' you couldn't get it up fer that fat shit-bag in a million years, ugly as she is—"

"I can say with all certitude: that's *not* what I was thinking."

"—so just think about that angel-food-cake blonde whiles yer doin' it. A nut's a nut, brother. We fellas gotta get it whiles we can."

Rosser grabbed his bag and sighed. "I appreciate the elucidating discourse."

"Yeah, man, I just *love* the way you talk! Later, Hoss. I'll be seein' ya."

God in Heaven I hope not.

Rosser stepped off into bristling heat and humidity. The bus pulled away before a wake of dust. His worst fear was that the fat woman would be sitting in the shelter, waiting for the next bus, which was exactly what Rosser had to do unless he wanted to walk a mile-plus to town. *Maybe she lives here,* he thought. *Please, God, let it be so that she's NOT waiting for the next bus. Let it be so that she's already walking home.*

God did not oblige his plea.

"Howdy, handsome," Maxine said, plopped fat and sassy in the shelter. The baby remained hooked to her side, dirty foot sticking out.

"Ga!" the baby blabbered. "Ga-Ga!"

"Uh, hello," Rosser had no choice but to respond. "I . . . presume you're . . . waiting for the . . . next bus?"

"Shore am, just like you. You live in Luntville?"

"Yes."

"Well, I do too! And we ain't got but a half hour to wait for the bus."

Jesus Christ! A half hour? "That's . . . not too long."

Rosser elected not to sit down next to her. She was truly hideous. Moles sticking out, plump fat face shiny in sweat, alcoholic nose like a strawberry. The elephantine thighs filled up the hem of the sundress to the extent that the material looked fit to rip. Corns pebbled the sunburned feet in dowdy flipflops, and tufts of hair, like Brillo, sprouted from her armpits.

"I'm Maxine," she said. "But I'se shore that character Corey told ya all about me."

Yeah, a ten-dollar prostitute. "Um, a little."

"Well, good, 'cos I gotta say I had my eye on you since I stepped on the bus. You're about the handsomest thang I seen in a while. What I mean is we can make a deal."

Rosser felt dead standing there. He didn't want to talk. He didn't want to be in any proximity at all to this woman.

"Oh, say hi to my darlin' little boy," and then she held her baby up. It was the first time Rosser got a direct look at the infant, and—

He nearly gagged.

It was a fat baby—six months old, eight months, he wasn't sure—and the child's head looked twice as large as it should've been and was slightly warped from what Rosser assumed was some congenital affliction. Rolls of fat under the chin, around the neck, bulbous cheeks. Tiny beady mud-brown eyes seemed hidden in folds of still more fat. The baby's lips looked inflated, like a pink sucker, smeared with chocolate. Mucus crusted its nostrils. Saliva glazed its chin.

The baby even had some moles on his neck.

Rosser was not a man prone to profanity, but when he got a good look at the child, he thought: *That is the ugliest motherfuckin' baby I've ever seen in my fuckin' life . . .*

Then the baby looked dully up at Rosser and blew out a wad of bubbly, Pop-Tart-flecked spit.

"His name's Shots." The woman held the baby's hand up, puppeting it to wave.

"*Shots?*" Rosser had to question.

"Named the little fella that on account of that's what I spent the whole time drinkin' when I was pregnant." She giggled. "Shots of vodka mostly, and Black Velvet whiskey."

I guess that explains the warped head, Rosser concluded.

"Say hi to the nice man, Shots. Hi, Mr. Nice Man." The woman beamed. "Ain't he just the cutest li'l thing?"

It's a fucking abomination...

"Where you from, sweetie?"

"Uh, Utah," Rosser lied.

"Oh, wow! A Canadian! It's easy ta tell you're new in town. I'se kin tell by yer shirt. Guess you used to be a businessman, huh?"

"Used to be. Yes."

The baby, now, seemed to be glowering at Rosser. If disdain could possibly be conveyed at so young an age, this was it. A pudgy pinky picked a booger from its nose and wagged it at Rosser. The other hand picked at a neck-mole.

"But back to what I was sayin'," Maxine continued. She munched on a Pop Tart as she spoke, crumbs on her lips. "Bein' that you're such a fine-lookin' man, I'll give ya a deal, a sweet one."

Rosser just stood there, numb. He looked appalled at the baby.

"I'll give ya a blow-job right here—a fine one, at that—fer just twenty-dollars."

"No. Thank you."

A coy smile. "Oh, I know, just like all men. Playin' hard ta get. You wanna see the goods first."

"Oh, no, that's really not nec—"

But already she'd pulled a breast out from her top: wide as a dinner plate, and flat. Rosser thought of a pita bread with a nipple. The nipple had several wire-like hairs sticking out of it. She flapped it for him, as though he'd find the gesture enticing.

"Wanna see my pussy, too? Here, take a peek—"

"No no no, really that won't be nec—"

She traversed her bulk on the bench, pulled her knees up, and there it all was: a quagmire of rank flesh and hair. If anything, the monstrous gash looked like a wound, brownish folds around a pucker. As much as Rosser tried to avert his eyes, some cruel and arcane impulse wouldn't allow it. He stared into the horror. At the nexus was a hole that glimmered within a rooster-wattle majora, and as if on cue a string of what could only be semen oozed out. The image came to mind: a toothless old man drooling.

"Oh, don't mind that little bit'a nut. Ain't no different from yours. Don't know why guys get the heebie-jeebies 'bout another fella's come. It's just fluid. You kin fuck me right here fer, say, thirty."

"No. Thank you."

"All right, Mr. Hard To Get. Twenty. And ya ain't gotta use a rubber 'er nothin' like that. I'm clean."

Oh, I'm sure. Pristine. Immaculate. Rosser just said, "No, thank you. I, uh, I don't have any money."

She maintained her poise, her knees aloft. The baby, meanwhile, greedily sucked at the broad, flat bag of skin that was her breast. The woman's knees looked like beaten faces. Now, that string of semen was dangling.

"Aaaaaall right," she conceded. "Since yer so good-lookin', you kin fuck me fer free. But'cha gotta eat my pussy first. Deal?"

At this, Rosser nearly laughed. *Lady, I would commit suicide before I would perform the act of cunnilingus on you. That's right. I would BLOW MY FUCKING HEAD OFF.*

"No. Really. Not today," was the only response he could summon that wouldn't be entirely rude.

Another sigh. "You drive a hard bargain." She finally lowered her mammoth legs. The visual nightmare, at least, was over. "Ten bucks and I'll blow ya. I don't get my welfare check fer two more weeks. I got rent ta pay and a kid ta feed. And I don't mind tellin' ya, I give a *damn* good blow-job."

Rosser was a reasonable man, but even the most reasonable men would, on occasion, err. The woman was hideous. There was NOTHING about her that could be described as erotic. And her kid was so fucking ugly Rosser thought he could bend over right now and throw up in the wire waste-can bolted to the bus shelter. But then he thought: *Well, she is poor. She does have a hard life. It's not her fault she's hideous. And the only reason she solicits sex is because she needs the money for her kid. I haven't had an orgasm in a month, and orgasms do indeed feel good. In fact, my genetics urge me to have orgasms—I can't help it. Fellatio does feel better than masturbation—a lot better—and to tell you the truth, I could kind of go for some of that right now. Like Corey said, a nut's a nut. And by doing this, I'd be helping her in a small way, making her very hard life a little bit easier. So—yes—I will go along with that theorem. A nut's a nut. I don't have to look at her. I'll do what Corey said. I'll close my eyes and think about that hot blonde, and you know what? It'll probably be pretty good.*

Rosser said, "Okay."

Maxine's pudding-face rejoiced. She jiggled her kid. "Did you hear that, Shots? Mr. Nice Man is gonna give us a ten-spot. Ain't that nice'a him?" She waved the kid's pudgy hand again. "Say thank you, Mr. Nice Man. Thank you, Mr. Nice Man!"

Jesus Christ . . .

"Any time yer ready, hon."

Rosser looked sheepishly down each side of the road. It was perfectly straight and perfectly deserted. He could see a mile each way. If anyone drove by, he'd be able to hear them long before they got close enough to see what was going on.

It's no big deal . . .

Maxine remained seated; Rosser stepped up. His penis felt numb, it felt like a small, shriveled up twig of flesh incapable of registering sensation—due to the recent assault of unwholesome imagery—but Rosser knew he could fix that.

He'd just close his eyes and think about the blonde.

He unbuckled his pants and lowered them and his briefs to his knees.

"Ooo, sugar, that's right. Just put it right in Maxine's face. I'll give you a cock-suck you'll never forget. But, I hate to tell ya this. Ain't ya forgettin' something?"

"Oh, yes, of course. The money. Sorry," he babbled and handed her a ten. She stuck it promptly into a pocket on her dress . . . and began to play with his testicles.

The grubby fingers were callused, not particularly pleasing, but then she began to run the tip of her tongue across his glans.

This gesture *was* particularly pleasing.

Rosser put his hands on his hips, leaned back a little. *Forget who's doing it. Just let it be done.* The frame of mind was working. He closed his eyes, thought about the blonde. It was the *blonde's* hand cupping his balls. It was the *blonde's* tongue laving circles around the rim of his penis. His erection sprang, hard as it had ever felt.

"Ga. Ga-ga. Ga."

Rosser opened one eye and looked down. The baby was grimacing up at him, still girded by his mother's arm. Where the infant's leg sprouted from the diaper, Rosser could see a line of shit. *Jesus Christ, the kid's diaper is full.* A big yellow piss stain was evident too.

"Ooo, honey, what's wrong?" the woman said in between sucks.

Rosser erection was losing a few notches. "Do, uh, do you think you could set the baby down? He's, uh . . . distracting me."

"Oh, Shots is just fine where he is—"

Rosser couldn't summon a way to say: *Look, if you don't mind, I'd prefer not to get my blow-job with my DICK a foot away from your kid! It's negligent! Mother's aren't supposed to suck dicks with their baby's watching! And the little fucker is staring right at me!* But he just didn't have it in him to say that. *Concentrate, concentrate!* Eyes closed again, his mind full of the blonde. *Yeah, yeah . . . Oh, man . . .* Those big, pouty lips, running up and down his shaft. Sun-blond hair tickling his thighs. Long tan fingers tracing his balls. Full turgidity returned an instant later. His hips began to quiver; his climax was just a few throbs away. And on the next stroke, just when Maxine drew her mouth back to his glans—

The baby grabbed his penis at the root.

"Jesus Christ!" Rosser winced, jerking away.

"What's wrong now, hon?"

What was wrong? "Your baby just grabbed my dick!"

The erection deflated.

"What're you all wound up fer?" Maxine asked. "He's just a li'l baby."

"Ga. Ga-ga." Then the baby picked his nose and tried to wipe it on Rosser's thigh.

"He's seen me givin' fellas head before, and fuckin' too. Ain't no big deal."

It's child abuse! Rosser pushed out his hand in abrupt jabs. "Look, look, *please.* Keep the baby's hands off me!"

"Awright, awright," she agreed, perturbed.

Of course, it would've been easier to just say to hell with it and walk off, but Rosser was pissed. He'd gone to a lot of trouble, a lot of annoyance (and a lot of revulsion) to get this far. He wasn't a quitter. He was bound and *determined* to have his orgasm. *Just put your dick back in her mouth, think about the blonde, and come!*

He put it back in. He thought about the blonde. He imagined her hands all over him. She was cooing in his ear, licking his neck, whispering adorations with her perfect bare breasts pressed against his chest. She was straddling him, her sex tight as a mouth itself, slowly drawing up and down over his erection. She was drenched, her own excitement for him undeniable. Now he was thrusting up, her breasts bouncing, her vagina clenching. She was sighing her bliss to the air, her eyes wanton slits.

Then she panted, "I love you, I love you . . ."

Rosser shuddered, ejaculating into the fantasy's loins which were actually Maxine's white-trash mouth. The semen blurted out of him, and now that he thought of it, it *was* very good oral sex.

Corey would've been proud of him.

Maxine pulled her mouth off. Had she swallowed? Rosser had heard no evidence of expectoration. When he looked at her, her expression seemed nonchalant, but . . . she kept her lips tightly seamed, as if deliberately holding his sperm inside. Post-climactic loss-of-breath diverted Rosser's focus; he wasn't paying much attention, but he was paying a little. Maxine, it seemed, continued to hold the semen in her mouth. Then she began to lean over—

What is she doing? it finally occurred to him.

—toward the baby.

As if on cue, the baby looked up, as though the strange gesture were familiar. Just as strangely, Rosser thought of a chick in a nest opening its beak when the mother landed with a worm.

The baby's fat-swaddled face beamed in elation.

Then its mouth opened.

Maxine brought her lips an inch from the baby's and began to--

Rosser slammed his eyes closed. *Oh my God, oh my God!* He would not allow himself to watch what he *knew* the mother was about to do . . .

"There, Shots!" she exclaimed. "Tum-tum full now?"

The initial shock locked him up; he was a root in the ground, in the cement. At first he didn't even believe what he'd seen. But when the baby—Shots—began smacking his lips with a big fat baby-smile, Rosser knew it was true.

"WHAT DID YOU DO!" he bellowed.

Maxine gave him the most absurd look, as though she'd done virtually nothing out of the ordinary. "It's just come. It's good fer him. He's a growin' boy and he needs to eat. I feed him all my trick's blow-jobs, just like my mama done fer me, and my daddy too." That look on her face lengthened. "Mister, you are one weird guy."

Rosser's shock persisted. He frantically yanked his pants back up. "It's child-abuse, for God's sake, if the county child-protection services knew—" but then his complaint was severed, by two things: One, a wet *splat!* and, two, something impacting his chest. Well, make that three: the unmistakable smell of human feces.

"HEY!" he shouted and jumped back. He glared at the baby.

Glossy strings dangled off the kid's chin. Shots grinned at him—a grin that could only be described as *evil*. The child had scooped some excrement out of the diaper and flung it on Rosser.

Maxine chuckled. "Oh, he's such a li'l devil, ain't he? Always throwin' his poop around."

Rosser stood aghast. The waste wasn't particularly solid, more like warm chocolate pudding, or mousse. Creamy. Smacking noises caught his attention next. He looked at Shots again and saw his little fingers playing with a few strings. The kid cackled greedily, then pointed a spermy finger at Rosser.

"Ga! Ga-ga!"

I'm . . . absolutely . . . mortified, Rosser thought.

Maxine was grinning at him, but it was a lascivious grin if anything. She was tweaking her nipples through her top. "I gotta tell ya somethin', handsome. Suckin' dick makes me horny as a bitch in heat, and after that blow-job, I am ALL fired up fer you. Git them pants back down. I'll get'cha hard again in a jiffy, then you's kin fuck me."

Rosser's shoulders slumped as if his collarbones had turned to rubber. "You're kidding me, right?"

"Does it look like I'm kiddin', cutie? Come on, I'se serious. No charge, neither." She looked at him and licked her lips. She pulled her knees back up, raised her hem, and bared the entire nightmarish mess that was her vagina. "Come'n get it."

"There is *no way.* There is no circumstance that exists on the surface of the earth that could compel me to have sex with you."

She blinked, uncomprehending. "Huh?"

"Let me put it another way, since you clearly don't understand the English language. I would rather *die* than put my dick in you."

Another blink, then the obese face reddened. When she lowered her knees, her big, corn-riddled flipflopped feet smacked the cement. The baby started crying.

"You ain't got no right to be so shitty ta me!" she railed, her voice rising. "I'm a respected woman round these parts—"

Rosser rolled his eyes.

"—and I won't stand fer bein' treated like that. So you git down on yer knees right now'n fuck me!"

"That won't be happening," Rosser said, nose crinkling at the shit-smell from his shirt. "That's an impossibility."

"Then gimme more money!" she demanded.

"No. I already gave you money."

"Why you prick! You asshole!" she began, her face nearly crimson now. The baby was crying in force, in machine-like bursts.

"Who do you think you are!" Maxine continued, "treatin' me like common tramp!"

Rosser rolled his eyes.

"Well, I'll show you, I'll show you—"

"Yeah, yeah," Rosser said. *She's flaking out. I'll just leave. It'll only take me a half hour to get back to Luntville.* He picked up his dollar-store bag, turned to leave—

"Oh, yeah, I'll fix your wagon, buddy." Now she was on her feet, the baby left to squall on the bench. "You just watch."

She bumbled toward him, flipflops snapping, tits jumping. At first Rosser thought she was going to assault him, but instead she edged out of the shelter, maniacal. Rosser just stared at her.

"What are you doing?" he asked.

She stood in the middle of the vacant road, waving at something. That's when Rosser noticed that the vacant road wasn't vacant anymore

The next bus was coming.

Maxine ludicrously jumped up and down in the road, waving her hands. Each time she landed, her fat jiggled in ripples.

"Help! Help! Hurry!"

Rosser was totally off guard. "What-what are you doing?"

"Help! This man molested my l'il baby!"

WHAT! "I didn't do anything of the sort!" Rosser shrieked at her. "You're the one who spit my semen in his mouth! Stop it!"

"Help! Hurry! Child molesterer! Child molesterer!"

146

The bus was getting real close, and the driver would have a radio. *And call the police,* he realized. "Just stop it! Here, here, I'll give you more money—"

"Fer-GET it, ya prick. I'm gonna fuck you up!"

Rosser tried to calm down. If he ran away, it would appear to the driver and passengers—material witnesses—that Rosser was guilty. If he stayed and stood his ground to dispute the allegation, he'd be more credible than she, right?

Then he looked at the baby. Shots was sitting back up in the shelter, waving pudgy arms and flinging more excrement. But his little fat and thoroughly atrocious face told all. Cloudy white blobs were still ringing his mouth.

Fuck!

Rosser ran.

The area seemed so wide open but then he noticed a decline off the road. He trotted down. He dared jerk his gaze behind him and saw the bus had already stopped, the driver and several rather rough-looking passengers coming out the door as Maxine wailed, "He molested my baby, my poor li'l Shots, right here in the shelter. I tried to stop him but he said he'd kill me—"

Oh, that's just terrific! Rosser thought.

"Jerked off right in my baby's face, he did!"

"Look at that! Damn if she ain't right," a passenger exclaimed. "Poor kid's face is covered with jizz—"

"I'm calling the police," the driver yelled and went back in the bus.

"Ain't gonna be no need fer no police," another, bigger, passenger assured, "not if we find this sick fucker first—"

"There! There he is!" Maxine shouted. She pointed right to Rosser, who was in the decline but his head showing. "Get him! Make him pay fer the horrible crime he done to my baby!"

Several figures began to run after him. Rosser hightailed it faster than he ever had in his life.

Lower into the decline, the woods began. He thrashed through brambles, leapt over tree stumps, tore through the forest. Deeper, it occurred to him that he had no idea where he was going, only a general inclination of direction. It also occurred to him, quite quickly, that he was not in the greatest physical condition. His heart hammered, he grew winded, and his knees and ankles began to ache—*My God, I've got to rest!*—but a surge of adrenalin dumped into his blood when he heard more thrashing behind him, the rapid footfalls of several men.

"Daggit, Jory. I'se think I see the monster, right down yonder past them trees!"

"Shore's shit do, Judd! We'se'll tune that sick bastard up *real* good!"

If those hayseeds catch me, they'll lynch me right here in the woods! Rosser kept running.

The tear through the woods seemed endless. As he progressed he felt more and more lost; he'd deliberately been zigzagging, hoping to lose them. Spider webs stretched across his face, bugs covered him, including masses of mosquitoes. At one point he slipped on something and fell flat on his face: a rotten woodchuck. At another point, when he thrashed through some vines, a yard-long green snake fell on him. Somehow, though, he managed to fling it off without shrieking. Within these woods, the humidity doubled, sucking sweat out of his skin.

Rosser kept running.

He stopped when it felt as though his heart would pop, leaned behind a tree. He wheezed in deep breaths that simply didn't seem to suffice; for a few seconds he feared he might pass out from exhaustion. The most dreadful notion told him that he'd soon be able to hear his pursuers, gaining on him, strong, young men, men who weren't winded at all but instead bent on vengeance.

Please, please, God. Don't let them get me, or if they do, please let it be quick . . .

Hugging the tree, he held his breath.

Listened.

Nothing.

Thank God . . .

His pursuers had branched off in the wrong direction. A few shouts in the distance verified the absolving observation: the shouts were getting further and further away, until they disappeared.

Yes, yes. Thank God.

Finally, luck seemed to be on his side. Another thirty yards through the woods showed him an open field beyond the trees, and the modest valley in which Luntville had been built. When he squinted he could even see Mrs. Doberman's rooming house!

Twenty-minute walk and I'm home!

It would be difficult, but he thought he could make it. He couldn't stay in town, of course, not with crazy Maxine accusing him of child molestation, but with just a little more luck, he could get in the house, get into his room and retrieve his money, then slip out again and hike to the next town and catch a bus somewhere else.

It was the only plan he had and it didn't sound too bad. Maxine had been the only one to see him, and he hadn't told her his name, nor his address. *I'll get my money and run,* he reasoned. *And I'll NEVER solicit a prostitute again!*

He was just about to exit the woods when sharp voices rose. He jumped to the ground behind a fallen log.

The voices blared with rage and urgency. Male voices.

"Kin ya believe the sick shit that people do?"

"Shee-it, brother. A baby, a little *baby!*"

The voices . . . were grimly familiar.

The Harkins boys.

The quadruplets . . .

"Maxine even said he butt-fucked the baby!"

Rosser nearly pissed in his jeans.

"Yeah, boys, he's one sick piece of shit, but if he thinks *he's sick* . . . we'll show him sick . . ."

"Yeah, man!"

All Rosser could think after that were two things:

A mallet-job . . .

And a dick-snagglin' . . .

"Bet he went in the woods. Let's go!"

No!

"Naw, why would he do that? Bet he went up the main road, to hitch a ride."

Yes, yes!

"Anybody know what the fucker looks like?"

"Naw, not his face 'er nothin'. Shouldn't be hard ta spot though, 'cos Maxine said he was wearin' a button-down white shirt."

"Come on, yer right. Let's head to the main road—"

Rosser let out the longest sigh of relief when they stomped off. Luck kept blessing him, that or God. He'd most easily be recognized by his shirt (which still reeked of infant excreta, by the way) but he still had his dollar-store bag, with t-shirts in it.

He changed shirts, waited until the Harkins boys were gone, and crept back to town.

Just act like everything's cool, he thought when he got back to the house. Not enough time had gone by for police to begin canvassing the neighborhood for the "child molester." Rosser did a competent job method-acting once he was back inside. Speaking briefly to other boarders, smiling and nodding, acting as thought nothing were out of the ordinary. No one gave im a second glance.

Once he'd returned to his room, he thought strategically. He'd leave town with a bare minimum—not that he'd arrived with much—but it made the most sense. The money he'd stolen from the company safe and the clothes on his back were all he needed. *I'll just go somewhere else, somewhere far from here.* Florida, perhaps, or Texas. It wouldn't take long. *And I'll wait till dark, easier get out of Luntville, lower visibility. Yeah, then hitchhike out and get a bus.* He'd simply start again, this time having learned his lesson.

He showered and changed, put the money in an innocuous bag, and at about nine p.m., left the room.

Another tenant greeted him as they passed on the stairs, an old man. "Night's coolin' down, ain't it?"

"Yes, sir, it is." Rosser feigned a chuckle. "It's about time, too, hot as it was today."

The old man paused, "Oh yeah, I'se almost fergot. Mrs. Doberman was lookin' fer ya."

Rosser almost shuddered. *Careful, careful!* But he knew he was also prone to overreacting. "Really? I saw her this morning. Any idea what she wants?"

"Naw. She's down in her office right now, though."

"I'll . . . go see her. Thanks."

This was something Rosser didn't need. But he still kept his cool. *If I sneak out without seeing her, that could definitely raise suspicion.* It was probably nothing, though. *She probably just wants to ask about next week's rent, wants to know how long I intend to stay. I'll pay next week's rent now. Then no one'll know I'm gone.*

He walked stolidly downstairs, through the day room to the office. The office door was open.

Rosser cleared his throat and entered.

"Oh, Mr. Rosser! There you are!" the landlady greeted from behind her desk. "I was just about to go to bed."

Mrs. Doberman had what could be described as a "hatchet-face." Mid-fifties, paunchy, graying hair pulled back in a bun. Through her tacky blouse, her breasts seemed to hang down to her stomach in tubes. Not a becoming woman, in other words, and–now that he thought of it . . .

She's almost as ugly as Maxine. Jesus. Must be something in the water.

"One of the other tenants said you wanted to talk to me."

"Why, yes." A big bright smile. "I just wanted to let you know that I didn't call the police."

151

Rosser's heart nearly stopped. He stared.

The ungainly woman stood up, came around the desk, and traced a crabbed, veiny hand across his shirt. "I couldn't do that. Selfish, call it."

Rosser croaked: "Puh-police."

"Of course. See, I know what you did. Molestin' that poor baby. Shame on you, Mr. Rosser!"

Rosser's throat felt like it was sealing shut. "I-I-I was set-up. I didn't do it, I swear to God. This-this woman I met on the bus . . . She made the whole story up."

She walked around, closed the office door, and locked it. Then she returned and sat up on the desk.

"Woman like me, gettin' on in her years, not much to look at no more? Then you walk in, the handsome stranger, so *different.* And on the run."

Rosser could not fathom this. "What . . . are you . . . talking about?"

The big stiff smile seemed to hover in the air. "Oh, I know that stuff about you messin' with the baby is all malarky—"

Rosser's eyes went wide. "You do?"

"Oh, shore, hon! Maxine told me all about it. She's always pullin' stunts like that. What a character! But don't you worry none. You take care'a me, and I'll take care'a you."

God Almighty! Rosser thought. Now Mrs. Doberman had hoisted her skirt, revealing a panty-less pubis. She was masturbating right there on the desk, her finger roving a vagina that was as much of a repulsive mess as Maxine's.

"You give me a some lovin' when I need it, and everything'll be fine," she said. "Oh, and just so ya know, what I like best is ta have my pussy et."

Rosser's mind spun. *Nightmare,* he thought but he knew he was awake. Then he remembered what she'd just said: *Maxine told me all about it.*

Rosser's voice grated like millstones. "You know Maxine?"

"A'course! She's my daughter, and she just moved in here with cute li'l Shots. Hey, Maxine?"

A door behind him clicked open, and in flopped Maxine, all smiles, all hanging fat and bulbous face and mole-studded neck. Now that he considered it, he easily saw the resemblance between the two women.

"Hi, there, Mr. Nice Man!" she celebrated. "Bet'cha thought ya'd never seen me again!"

The atrocious baby remained wrapped around her side. It glared at him, blowing spit bubbles.

"Ga! Ga-ga!"

"Git down on them knees, Mr. Rosser," the landlady instructed, "and give me some proper pussy-eating. Once or twice a day's all I'll need. And each time yer done with me, ya kin have some fun with Maxine, too. Way I understand the law, there ain't no expiration'a the time Maxine can press charges against ya fer child-molestation."

Rosser was growing dizzy in nauseousness. Mrs. Doberman spread her legs, dividing her sloppy vulva with her finger.

"So come on, you silly man. Let's git on with it!"

Rosser fell to his knees.

"And when you're done with Momma," Maxine added, "I'll be in the bedroom, waitin' on ya."

Shots flapped some feces on Rosser's back.

"Ga! Ga-ga!" the baby said.

The McCrath Model SS40-C, Series S

"She'll have to eat it," Prouty said, "otherwise, she'll drown."

Vinchetti appraised the situation, a dark, if not bewildering, scrutiny. "You're one sick motherfucker, Doc—to think of something like this."

Hey, you're the one who insists on these little revenge skits, you stromboli-eating whack-job, thought Doc a.k.a. Dr. Winston F. Prouty. Fifty-seven years old, tall, lean, gray-templed, Dr. Prouty looked liked his former self in his clean white lab-coat and perfect posture. Deloreanesque, distinguished. Not too long ago, he'd been earning over a million a year as one of Beverly Hills' most prominent reconstructive plastic surgeons. Tit-jobs for the stars. Brad Pitt noses for every Brad Pitt wannabe in La-La Land. Doc had liposucked Nicholson five times, and had created enough Hollywood cleavage to rival the East African Rift. Posh office on Wilshire Boulevard, waterfront Malibu beach house, Lamborghini in the drive. It had only taken a year to lose it all—thanks to a high gambling marker with the mob . . . oh, and the demerol habit. Now Dr. Prouty worked for Vinchetti.

"It will, in the least, provide a captivating demonstration of the extremities of the human survival instinct," the doctor appended.

"Doc, I *love* the way you talk!" Vinchetti replied and smacked his hands together.

That's because I have an education, unlike you and your

goombah psychopaths. He tightened the straps on the lab table, checked the angle of the lights for the video camera. Vinchetti always wanted these little vignettes preserved on tape, for sale to his sickest clients, and to serve as reminders to his own people: This Is What Happens If You Fuck With Paul Vinchetti.

Indeed. It was.

Paul Vinchetti II was the supreme boss in what the U.S. Justice Department referred to as the Vinchetti/Lonna/Stello Crime Pyramid, an armature of that mythical human machinery known as the Mafia. When his father had died of a coronary while eating calamari and white pizza, Paul had taken over the entire ball of mob wax by waging war with the rest of the families. He had the muscle. Now he controlled all of the white heroin distribution on the east coast, as well as underground porn distribution, and, of all things, magazine distribution. Slowly but surely he was working his way west with gambling and black-market import interests. The gambling—that's how Dr. Prouty had gotten involved.

He'd run up a couple of hundred grand at the black-jack tables, and shortly thereafter had lost his license. (Two botched blepharoplastys in a row had left a corporate attorney's wife and a DreamWorks exec with insufficient blood-supply to the eyelids. Eventually, the eyelids had rotted off.) The lawsuits had taken everything, but that wasn't Prouty's biggest worry, and neither were the impending criminal charges for performing critical oro-facial surgery while under the influence of a pharmaceutical morphine derivative.

Unable to make his payments, Prouty knew Vinchetti's district boys would come a'callin', and when they did, they made him an offer he couldn't refuse. "We can hang you upside-down by a meat-hook through your asshole," they'd been kind enough to explain, "and then blow-torch you to death, or . . ."

"So how long's it take, Doc?" Vinchetti asked.

"Oh, twenty more minutes perhaps, before the copper sulphate adequately saturates the duodenal blood vessels."

"And where the hell's Tony?"

"I believe he's trying to locate a camera, sir."

"The fuck?" Vinchetti complained. "What's taking him so long? We got more cameras in this joint than Paramount. Jesus Christ."

"They were making some snuff tapes in the basement last night. Remember? The deputy police commissioner's children?"

The memory rekindled on Vinchetti's expression. "Aw, yeah, that's right—the baby triplets. I'll bet that's gonna be some sweet work."

Dr. Prouty frowned to himself. He remembered seeing the crew bring in the pit bulls.

A chuckle, then: "Teach that fuck cop to bust my guys," Vinchetti continued. "Fuckin' guy's been on our pad for five fuckin' years, and *now* he wants to break bad?" Another chuckle. "He'll know what bad is when he sees that tape."

Prouty felt a twinge in his belly, in spite of his now-well-honed clinical detachment. But getting back to his own predicament, when given the choice of hanging upside-down from a meat-hook in his rectum or working for Vinchetti, the doctor had unsurprisingly picked the latter. This involved an expeditious relocation to one of Vinchetti's compounds on the outskirts of Pennellville, New York. The facility was part safe-house, part recovery ward, and part full-tilt mother-fuckin' chamber of horrors. Its remote location made it perfect for all of the above, especially the video end. All manner of illegal and homicidal pornography was made on the premise: snuff flicks, nek flicks, "wet" S&M, and various other types of productions the likes of which could make even the lowest demon queasy. But Dr. Prouty had little to do with the videos; his chief purpose at the compound entailed changing appearances. Two weeks of cold-turkey withdrawal had cured him of his demerol addiction, after which he'd begun to utilize his clinical expertise in order to pay back his gambling debts. Whenever it was looking like the feds were going to grab one of Vinchetti's men cold, said man would come to the compound and, thanks to Prouty's skills, leave several weeks later with a new face. Simple. And Prouty didn't really mind at all. They gave him a little room to live in, three meals a day plus all the satellite channels, and it sure as hell beat hanging from that hook. Escape was impossible; the compound was constantly locked, full of guards, and close to a fifty miles from any other dwellings. It was this or the hook.

This worked.

These little side jobs were another matter, though. Not only was the compound used as a production stage for the most unimaginable endeavors in visual pornography, it was a stage, too, for Vinchetti's own personal desires for vengeance. Whenever somebody stole from Vinchetti, or lied to him, insulted him, slighted him in any way, it was Dr. Prouty's job to initiate a creative revenge which Vinchetti would personally witness and have video-taped for posterity. The deeds definitely tested Prouty's intestinal fortitude but then . . . there was always the hook . . . so he simply did what he was told and didn't morally question himself about the victims. Hell, they were all probably bad people anyway.

Quite often, Prouty kept them alive for as long as possible. Non-anesthetic lobotomies were another Vinchetti favorite, as were full body flensings, acid catheters, and "trunk jobs." Genital mutilation comprised so much activity in this place that it had actually grown blasé; you could only dissect some many penises, remove so many scrotums, poach so many testes, and gun-brush so many urethras before it lost its thrill. Hence, Vinchetti kept pressing the doctor for new and original spectacles.

Like this one.

The woman's name was Darcy, one of Vinchetti's part-time paramours. Vinchetti liked them skinny and trashy (such women reminded him of his New Jersey childhood) and Darcy definitely fit the bill. Ninety-five pounds, tiny-breasted, and with a mouth more foul than the bottom of a slaughter house dumpster, Darcy had made the faux pax of telling one of the other girls: "Vinch has a little dick. It's teeny, like my pinkie."

Big mistake.

The other girl had ratted and now here Darcy lay, side-strapped nude to Prouty's work table. It was an odd sight, to say the least: Prouty thought of conjoined twins connected at the mouth. See, Darcy shared the lab table with another of Vinchetti's employees, one Hymie Levy. Hymie was a young mathematics whizz-kid who'd graduated with honors from Georgetown Business School, and now—or it should be said, until very recently—he'd served as one of Vinchetti's accountants. Standing at a full five-foot four, Hymie weighed—easily—three hundred pounds, and the reason he occupied space on the torture table was simple: he'd been skimming money from Vinchetti's trough. Hence, the mandate. If you stole even a nickel from the boss, you got the table. It was the principle of the thing.

Vinchetti was wincing at the site of Hymie strapped naked to the table. "Christ, Doc, that's a lot of matzah balls; he looks even worse with his clothes *off.* The kid's got enough blubber on him to keep an Eskimo family eating for ten years. No wonder there's people starvin' in the world. This fat fuck ate all the food."

"I wouldn't be too hasty in accusing the obese of a lack of will-power," Dr. Prouty pointed out. "Recent research from John's Hopkins indicates that perhaps as much as forty percent of obesity in America can be attributed to a previously unidentified icosahedral virus. Nonstructural protomers in the viral shell allow it to roam undetected by immune responses and directly attack the mitochondrion mechanisms in human fat cells. The result is a cell that cannot effectively turn glucose into energy—hence, an excess storage of adipose matter. Obesity is a tragic disease, not an instance of willful over-indulgence."

"Aw, put a lid on that liberal bullshit, will ya, Doc? The fat motherfucker's fat 'cos he can't keep his fat fuckin' hands out of the fuckin' refrigerator. He eats six fuckin' meals a fuckin' day. He stuffs his fat motherfuckin' face every fuckin' chance he gets. It ain't no fuckin' *virus,* Doc. It ain't no fuckin' *disease.* The only problem this fat fuck has is a fuckin' fork-to-mouth problem."

Prouty knew the futility of taking exception. "Of course, you're quite correct, sir. Pardon my oversight."

Vinchetti smiled subtly. "Damn straight. And this fat fuck's definitely had *his* last fuckin' meal."

"Actually, sir," the doctor reminded, "if you give the matter some abstract consideration, they'll both be spending their final moments of life . . . eating with quite a bit of gusto."

Vinchetti's eyes dimmed for a second, then, "Oh, yeah! I get'cha, Doc! Man, is this gonna be sweet!"

Indeed, Prouty commiserated. Medium doses of Phenolax had rendered both subjects unconscious, after which Dr. Prouty had stripped them and strapped them, face to face, on the table.

Then he'd . . . connected them . . . at the lips.

Vinchetti was leaning over, peering at their faces. "So how'd you do their lips, Doc? What, you *stitched* 'em together? That looks like some pretty tough work."

It was actually the simplest chore of all; the only "tough" work was suitably arranging Hymie's incredible bulk on the table. "With this," Prouty said, and held the instrument up.

At first glance, one might think the doctor had raised a chrome-plated curling iron, or even an electric steak knife. A power cord led to a shiny oval-shaped housing which fit comfortably in Prouty's hand. From the front end protruded two very narrow steel tubules, whose gap could be adjusted by a knob at the base. "It's a McCrath Model SS40-C, Series S, top of the line."

"The fuck's that?" Vinchetti queried.

"It's a surgical stapler."

And a fine one at that. It functioned similarly to an ordinary office stapler, though its feed mechanism was much more intricate. The impact tubule, containing the foot-end, ran parallel to the loading tubule. The two objects to be coupled were merely fitted into the gap at the end of the device, and—*CLACK!*—the power button was applied. The ends were joined while a curvicular one-millimeter surgical-grade staple was fired and shunted to the foot-end—and anything between it. The instrument was mainly used for long lacerations over deep wounds and re-attaching mesenterial tissue during primary abdominal operations. In *this* case, however, it was providing a very new and creative utility.

"You *stapled* their lips together?" Vinchetti deduced.

"That's correct, sir. The entire procedure took less than a minute, I'd say."

Vinchetti stepped back, astonished. "That's really *neat-o!*"

Dr. Prouty rolled his eyes. *Yes. Neat-o.*

At the same moment, the door opened, and in walked Vinchetti's most trusted lieutenant, a weasel-faced little man with hair like steel wool and more pock-marks than Tommy Lee Jones. Tony Guerini had worked his way up from the bowels of Trenton. As a kid, he'd bagged for the numbers racket in all the worst neighborhoods, and as a teenager he was working enforcement. When a hooker gypped her pimp, it was Tony who uglied her up, cutting off her clitoris for the first offense, her nose for the second, then the head for the third. When a numbers collector came up short, it was Tony who shattered his spine, and when a distro guy stepped on the smack a little too hard, it was Tony who cranked the tourniquet around his neck till his eyeballs popped half out and his face hemorrhaged. Tony was an industrious young man. And by the age that most young men were graduating college, Tony was proving himself as a most reliable "button" for the Vinchetti Family. He deemed no job too abhorrent, no hit contract too deplorable. Be it a hardened crew-boss from a rival family or an eighty-year-old lady who was a crooked cop's mom, Tony would tear out the heart of the crew-boss with a claw hammer and rape the old lady to death without so much as a blink. He'd once machine-gunned an entire busload of first graders simply because one of the kids was a judge's grandson, and when the Catholic diocese had threatened to not pay back their loan, it was Tony who kidnapped those three nuns from St. Christopher's and . . .

Well . . .

You don't really want to know what he did to them.

It should suffice to say, then, that Tony didn't tip-toe through the tulips when it came to getting family work done, and when the Paul Vinchetti had had to go to war, Tony was his commander in the field. A loyal friend and most trusted adjutant.

"Tony!" exclaimed Vinchetti with enthusiasm. "Where ya been, my man! The fun's about to start!"

"Wouldn't miss it for a cock-suck from Jenna Jameson," Tony replied, sporting a high-end Sony Max-Cam. Then he took a look at Hymie's bulbous hairy buttocks. "Er, on second thought, maybe I would."

Vinchetti honked comradly laughter and slapped his friend on the back. "Aw, come on! Big bad tough-guy human meat-grinder like you? You'll *love* this!"

Tony (who, by the way, wore an absolutely ridiculous white suit, black satin shirt, and red tie) screwed the camera onto a Vivitar tripod. "Fuckin' Hymie," he muttered. "I told ya, boss. I told ya that tub'a shit was skimming some cream off the top."

"Yeah," Vinchetti remarked. "I had Lunky put a hidden camera in the cash room. Got the walrus-lookin' fat scumbag rippin' me off *on tape*."

"How much did he pinch? Couple hundred large?"

"Fuck, no. Twenty bucks. It ain't the amount, ya know? It's the deed. Ya gotta be loyal in this business."

Tony nodded sternly. "Damn straight."

Dr. Prouty, meantime, stood aside, barely listening to the wise-guy banter. He hoped they could get on with it soon. *Emeril Live* came on in an hour. *Bam!*

Now Tony was widening the hoods on the lights. "So when did ya tell him you had him cold?"

Vinchetti's slick grin turned up higher. "This morning right after breakfast. You should'a seen him, Tony! He put down four plates of hash and eggs, so then me and Knuckles Jr. bring him into the office, show him the tape. He was blubberin' like a baby—a *giant* baby!—and he's on his knees beggin' for his life, kissin' my wing-tips. Thought he was gonna upchuck all that food right there on the carpet." Vinchetti's eyes took on a glitter. "And it's a good thing he didn't 'cos . . ."

But Tony's attention had drifted to the broad lab table where Hymie and Darcy lay strapped. He squinted in confusion. "Who's that there strapped next to him? Darcy?"

"Yeah, she mouthed off," Vinchetti explained. "Didn't know a good thing when she saw it, if ya know what I mean. Kind'a hate to see her go, though. Flap-jacks for tits and a pussy on her about useless—you could stick a magnum of Asti Spumanti up there and there's *still* be slack—but, *man,* could she chug a cock. I'll tell ya, Tony, she'd have my rod in her yap right down to the root and *still, somehow* she'd be able to tongue my asshole."

"'S'shame to have to deep-six a talent like that."

Vihchetti made an odd pause. "Well, you know what I'm talkin' about, Tony. Right?"

"What'cha mean, boss?"

"Yeah, sure. I heard she's been blowin' you all along, same time she was blowin' me. Heard you were fuckin' her too."

Tony shot a dark glance right back. "Hey. Boss. Jokin' around like that ain't funny. I would never, and I mean *never,* fuck around with your private stock."

"Yeah?"

"Yeah," Tony said.

Vinchetti eyed his friend a moment more, then cracked his hands together and burst out laughing. "Hey, Doc! Would ya get a load of this guy? He thought I was *serious!*" Vinchetti slapped Tony hard on the back, still honking laughter.

Dr. Prouty rolled his eyes.

"Yeah, boss, you're a real comedian," Tony said.

"Bet'cha about shit yer pants, huh! Naw, Tony, I know you'd never fuck me over; I was just funnin' with ya. But this crackhead bitch here—she's got a good one comin'."

"So what she mouth off about?"

"Can ya believe it? The little spunk rag said that I . . ." Vinchetti thought the better of elaborating. "She just got mouthy, you know?"

"Sure. Ain't nothin' worse than a split-tail who don't know her own place. Only time a chick's mouth should be open is when someone's got a hard-on to stick in it. Rest of the time it should be closed."

Dr. Prouty nearly blanched. *I have a feeling these two don't make any charitable donations to the National Organization of Women.*

"I hear that," Vinchetti agreed. "And what do guys like us do every time? Give 'em some green, put some nice jewelry around their skinny necks, and then they start to think they're special. They start to get uppity. Start mouthin' off, start gripin' and takin' you for granted. Well fuck that shit."

Tony nodded in this deep philosophical unanimity. "Fuckin' chicks. Ain't none of 'em no good when ya get down to it. Ain't nothin but a bunch of cum drains, boss, a bunch of low down dirty whores." But Tony flinched immediately after he'd spoken the words. "Er, what I mean is all of 'em except your wife, boss."

A laudable exclusion, Prouty thought.

Vinchetti returned the nod. "Well, yeah. Right."

"So what'cha got planned for these two?"

"Oh, it's a doozy, Tony! Doc here came up with the idea. Take a look, take a *close* look at 'em."

Tony leaned closer over the two immobile faces. "Looks like .

.. What the hell? Looks like they're stuck together somehow . . . by their lips."

Vinchetti chuckled. "Yeah, ain't it neat-o? Doc here's got this machine that stapled their lips together."

"It's a McCrath Model SS40-C," Dr. Prouty piped in, holding the device up. "From their 'S' series, 'S' for small. It's quite a quality item. The adjustable impact and foot assemblies allow for a—"

"Shaddap," Vinchetti said, turning his attention back to Tony. "Ain't that somethin'? Ain't that some work?"

Tony continued to examine the fine details of the "work" with a watch-maker's study. "You ain't kiddin'. But . . . I don't get it. They ain't dead already, are they?"

"Naw, just unconscious. Doc here shot each up with some heavy duty tranks."

"Actually," the doctor interjected, now holding up his Bush automatic syringe, "I used the latest barbituric-acid derivative, Phenolax. Induces total unconsciousness in less than twenty seconds. It works by reducing the biogenic output of the diazamine receptors in the brain and—"

"Shaddap," Vinchetti ordered, then said back to Tony, "And they'll be coming to in a few minutes—that's when the fun begins. Remember what I said about Hymie, right? The fat hump plowed down *four plates* of hash and eggs for breakfast, and I'm talkin' *stacked* plates, Tony. I'll bet this kid's got five pounds of grub in his belly, and now Doc's gonna make him throw it all up."

Tony's minor powers of calculation ticked for a moment, then he saw the ploy. "Aw, boss, that's low down. He'll be puking it all up right into Darcy's mouth."

"That's the plan. Slick, huh? And shell have to scarf up all that puke and fast, or else she'll kick, right Doc?"

"That's correct, sir," Prouty replied. "Once Hymie begin's to aspirate the vomitus, it will have no place to go but into Darcy's oral cavity, and due to the obvious fact that their mouths are surgically adhered, Darcy will need to swallow it all as quickly as it is disgorged. If she does so, she'll survive; however, if the volume of the regurgitant exceeds her capacity to swallow it, her tracheal passage will become obstructed, whereupon the vomit will congest in the upper bronchi. As I was remarking to Mr. Vinchetti earlier. She'll have to eat it, or she'll drown."

Vinchetti cracked his hands together. "Damn! Ain't it great the way Doc talks?"

Tony's brow furrowed in an expression of deep admiration. "I *like* it. The skinny bitch drowns in Hymie's hash and eggs." Then he scratched his head. "But how are you gonna make him puke?"

"Doc just injected him with this fancy stuff," Vinchetti answered.

"A simple saline and copper sulphate solution injected intra-muscularly," Doc said. "Once the compound comes in sufficient contact with the stomach's exterior blood supply—"

"Shaddap," Vinchetti said. "Just take his word for it, Tony. It won't be long before Hymie's blowin' chunks like a fuckin' bilge pump."

"You figure she'll be able to do it?" came Tony's next query. "You know, eat all that puke?"

Both mobsters considered the rather remarkable question. "What do you think, Doc?" Vinchetti asked, chuckling. "I mean, seein' that you're a gambling man, if you had money to bet, would you bet she could do it?"

"I would, sir," Dr. Prouty responded in certainty. "The primal instinct for a human being to survive is unfathomably spirited. In fact, I'd say she'll survive several cycles."

"Cycles?" Tony asked.

Vinchetti explained. "See, if the bitch manages to swallow all that puke, then Doc injects *her* with some of that fancy copper stuff. Get it? Then it's *her* turn to puke into *Hymie's* mouth. They'll just keep puking back and forth like that till they croak."

"That rocks!" Tony exclaimed.

Prouty noticed a gradual increase in respiration in the victims. Eyelids began to flutter. "If I may interrupt, sir. I believe our subjects are regaining consciousness."

"Tony! Turn on the camera," Vinchetti made the zealous command. "Get us a wide shot, the whole table. I want to see 'em convulsing'n shit."

Tony did so, and soon the convulsing began. First, though, came the initial recognition of the calamity. Hymie and Darcy's eyes did indeed flutter open. They stared glazily for a few seconds . . . and then the rest hit them: they were strapped to each other, face to face, irrevocably joined at the lips.

Then they began to scream into each others mouth.

The sounds were muffled, of course, more like a panicked mewling, Hymie's lower, in staccato-like gruffs, Darcy's a long high baffled whistle. It was a sound unlike any Dr. Prouty had ever heard. An additional leather strap girding their necks prevented any possible action to pull back and tear out the staples. The victims squirmed within their bonds, bug-eyed, trying to kick, frenetically jerking, trying to somehow twist out—but each and every gesture proved futile.

All three men stood stock-still, watching raptly. A considerable erection became evident at the front of Tony's preposterous white slacks, but Vinchetti himself seemed to be growing bored. "Hey, Doc. We got video runnin' here, ya know, and we ain't got till fuckin' Christmas. When's Hymie start to let 'er rip?"

Prouty felt a few pops of sweat come out on his brow. "It used the maximum human dose, I assure you, sir. Given Hymie's greater than average capillary tract, due to the excess of fat, the vomitive compound may take a trifle longer than expected to reach the target duodenal blood vessels. You see, sir, a person such as Hymie— clinically obese—actually possesses a higher volume of hemoglobin due to the fact—"

"Shaddap," Vinchetti said. "Just make him puke, Doc. If that

166

sack'a blubber ain't pukin' in five minutes, I'll have my boys hang you upside-down from a meat-hook in your asshole. Savy?"

Dr. Prouty gulped through a nod as he spied the recurring image in his head.

"Shit, Tony," the boss went on, "this is makin' for some pretty dull footage. I think what we need is a little rodwork to spice things up while we're waitin' for Hymie to blow chow."

Tony popped a brow, half eyeing Darcy's quirming buttocks. "Yeah, boss, but you know, like I was saying before, I'd never fuck around with any of your squeeze."

Vinchetti cracked a laugh. "She ain't my squeeze no more, Tony. Shit, you think I give a shit now? Once we're done with the fun and games here, I'm gonna have Knuckles Jr. carve her up and put her in the grinder for the pit bulls. So go ahead, paisan. Use it or lose it."

Tony shrugged. "Don't mind if I do." He lowered his ludicrous slacks and zig-zag-patterned Fruit of the Looms, freeing a hard penis that looked more like an eight-inch length of knockwurst. He slicked it up via some spit in the palm and wasted no time getting it where he wanted it. As if Darcy's plight weren't regrettable enough–now this: perfunctory sodomy. She *really* began to squirm.

"And don't forget the wet shot," Vinchetti reminded. "After all, this is video."

"Got'cha, boss. When I'm done coring this stringbean, her ass is gonna look like a rum bun."

Since Darcy and Hymie were strapped face to face, her buttocks was positioned quite conveniently. All Tony need do was step right up and slip it in. Her whistle-like mewls heightened whilst Tony's frightfully thick member methodically plumbed the depths of her rectal passage.

Then Vinchetti looked over at Doc and said, "You too, Doc. Get on it."

Prouty froze. "Uh, pardon me?"

"Whip out your johnson and put it where the sun don't shine."

Prouty's mouth fell open but no words came out. A quick appraisal of the obvious (there were two naked asses on the table, and one was currently occupied) did not leave him with much of a positive conclusion. "Uh-uh-uh . . . you want me to-to-to—"

"That's right, Doc. Get your dick out, get it hard, and fuck Hymie in the ass. Jesus Christ, you act like I'm askin' you to build the Great Pyramid."

The doctor looked at Hymie's clenching buttocks. It was hairy . . . and huge. It lay there on the side of the table like one fifty-pound bag of flour stacked upon a second. Doc made the only logical response. "Uh-uh-uh . . . sir, I-I-I couldn't *possibly*—"

Like magic, Vinchetti shucked a small semi-automatic pistol and aimed it right at Prouty's face. "Come on, Doc. Chop chop. You know how I hate loud noises."

Prouty stood in total paralysis. "But, sir, given the sheer size of Hymie's buttocks, not to mention the considerable over-hang of flesh . . . I rather doubt that a . . . successful insertion . . . would even be physiologically possible."

Vinchetti cocked the pistol.

Oh, dear, Dr. Prouty thought. "As I said, I'll give it my most concerted effort, sir."

"That's the spirit."

Prouty could scarcely imagine a predicament such as this. Tony didn't seem to be having any trouble at all, but of course, for one thing, Tony was a demented sexual psychopath and, two, the lithe female derriere he so frenetically sodomized was a bit more pleasing to the erotic imagination than the corpulent mass that Prouty was tasked with. He lowered his trousers and briefs only to find his own penis so withered it appeared to be retracting into his body. *I'm going to put THIS,* he thought, and looked at Hymie's ass, *into THAT?*

The doctor remained locked in rigor.

"Look, Doc," Vinchetti said with an eerie calm. "Either you cornhole Hymie or I'll kneecap you and feed ya live to the pit bulls.

Now quit dilly-dallying. Get some shit on your stick."

A deep breath, then—capitulation. Dr. Prouty began to masturbate, standing right there with his trousers at his ankles. His penis felt like a piece of warm taffy (a *small* piece), and now his previous words were haunting him in a manner that he could scarcely conceive of. *The primal instinct for a human being to survive is unfathomably spirited,* he determined just moments ago. Well, here was his chance to prove that particular maxim.

Oh dear me . . . He could imagine how he appeared: huffing and puffing, knees shaking and eyes squeezed shut, hands plying a dead dick. The mewls of horror issuing from the table didn't exactly help him get in the mood. He reassembled any erotic image in his mind: Farrah Fawcett in *Playboy,* the models in the *Victoria's Secret* catalogue, and all those nut-brown, bikini-lined Beverly Hills bimbos he'd had on his own table not too long ago. He imagined Cindy Crawford's hand in place of his own, while Ginger from *Gilligan's Island* tended his testes with her tongue. The latter image was beginning to work until some devious mental glitch replaced Ginger with Gilligan himself.

Back to square one.

How about that nameless brunette from the Tobe Hooper flop *Lifeforce?* Ooo-la-la. And all those silly ditzes in those *Girls Gone Wild* video commercials? Better. When the doctor thought of Ellie May in her too-tight one-piece lounging by the cee-ment pond, he actually felt the inklings of, perhaps, legitimate vasocongestion. *It's working!* he thought. *It's working!* But, alas, a fraction of a second later, Jethro trundled into the image and all was lost again.

"Time's runnin' out, Doc. I'll give ya to the count of three."

The doctor wiped his mental slate clean. *Enough of that!* Instead, he put his fate simply into the hands of the human survival instinct.

"One."

I'll do it!

"Two."

Come on!

"Thr—"

Presto! The genuine threat of death did the trick, and no forced thoughts of voluptuous vixens were necessary. Before the doctor could worry any further, six hard-as-ever inches stuck out grandly.

"Three cheers for Doc!" Vinchetti celebrated. "Not bad for an old fuck!"

I'd duly flattered, Dr. Prouty thought.

"Now get that California balony pony where it belongs, and *don't* make me have to count to three again."

Dr. Prouty didn't expend precious time thinking; he merely followed Tony's fine technical example, spat into his hand, and transferred the all too critical lubrication to his erection. Then, with some effort, he pushed up the upper slab of Hymie's buttocks and—

Don't think about it! Don't think about it!

—slid his glans into the terrifying crevasse. Luck was on his side—for a change—as said glans found the area in question almost instantaneously: Hymie's rectal sphincter. Dr. Prouty urged his pelvis forward, felt some understandable resistence, then sighed in relief.

He was in!

"There ya go, Doc. Now give that fat shit a butt-fucking like his momma never dreamed."

It felt like the tightest of o-rings clamped around his penis. It did not feel good. Nevertheless, realizing his life was at stake he . . . butt-fucked the living daylights out of Vinchetti's unfortunate former accountant. An errant glance aside showed him that Tony was doing the same to Darcy as she continued in her whistle-like protests. The slaps of their groins to their subjects' rumps provided a bizarre stereoscopic sodomy. Tony was going hell for leather, and some inexpressible inclination caused Dr. Prouty to keep pace.

"Remember, boys," Vinchetti said, "I need wet shots. Spunk 'em both up good. Oh, and Doc? How's this for a deal? If you get your nut before Tony . . . I'll let ya go."

Dr. Prouty's heart surged at the pledge, then more survival instinct kicked in. No erotic imagery needed, no luxurious fantasy required to prompt the called-for effect. Deft as a porn star, the doctor withdrew his member and—

Ahhhhhhhhhhhhhhhh . . .

—fired half a dozen gouts of sperm a yard across the table.

"Holy shit, Doc!" Vinchetti cheered. "That's some serious baby-batter you're pumpin' out! Hey, Tony! The old geezer beat ya to the finish line, and—holy shit!—he just hosed 'em *both* down!"

This was a fact. Dr. Prouty's veritable *vault* of semen had not only plastered Hymie but Darcy as well. Like trails of egg-drop soup, the viscid lines lay across their sides. One shot even made it to Darcy's left ear.

Prouty leaned back against the wall, too exhausted to even pull his pants back up. Inside, though, he beamed. He'd *done* it.

"I'm proud of ya, Doc," Vinchetti said, "and I'm a man of my word, so don't you worry. But we still got a little more to do before you go waltzing out of here."

"Of course, sir. Thank you, sir."

I'm free! Prouty thought. *I'm finally going to get to leave this hell hole!*

The thumping from the table intensified; Tony was reaching his own moment of crisis, care of Darcy's throttled rectum. The stainless steel examination platform actually shook from the concluding strokes. Then—

"Here's one for the Gipper, bitch—"

Tony too demonstrated an impressive ejaculation, spackling Darcy's clenched, moon-white bottom until it sufficiently shined.

"Good cum-shots, boys, *real* good," Vinchetti praised.

Tony's cheeks billowed as he let out a long breath. "All in a day's work." Then he looked down at his slackening penis. "Hey, boss, how do you like that? Clean peter, not a speck'a shit on it."

"Yeah, these crackheads, ya know? They barely eat nothin'," the boss eloquently pointed out.

Prouty, when he dared look himself, wasn't nearly as lucky. His penis was *caked* with feces; he even noted a tell-tale piece of corn. Embarrassed, he quickly rebuckled his pants before the others could notice.

He'd . . . clean up later.

Vinchetti shot him a glance. "Okay, Doc, now that you've had your fun, when's the puke party gonna start?"

It was a reasonable question. Both subjects continued to mewl, writhing within their bonds. Dr. Prouty knew that if he didn't get this show on the road, all previous bets—i.e., his freedom—were off, and he knew what the problem was: sheer physical mass . . . He prepared another injection of the copper sulphate—ten times the recommended maximum human dose. A dose this large would cripple liver and pancreatic function as well as cause considerable brain damage but . . .

Hymie won't need any of that, the doctor realized. *All Hymie needs to do is vomit.*

And vomit Hymie did—in grand style—less than a minute after the second injection. Much gastric turbulence preceded the event—sounds akin to a fish tank—and then came the salvo of muffled retches. Lip-locked, Hymie and Darcy's eyes shot wide open, their faces turning red, their limbs suddenly seized by shock.

That's the ticket, Prouty thought in relief.

Hymie's fat cheeks ballooned, then the retching deepened, and after that, a simplicity of molested nature took its inescapable course.

"Here comes lunch!" Vinchetti shouted in glee.

Even the doctor, in the most abstract of notions, found the atrocious exhibition to be strangely fascinating. One stomach emptying into another. Food consumed previously being ejected into an adjacent mouth only to be consumed again. It was the ultimate in recycling.

Vinchetti and Tony hooted and hollered like a pair of riotous fans at a football game. All the while, Hymie continued to throw up into Darcy's mouth, and Darcy—little trooper that she was—continued, somehow, to swallow each hot, chunky gust. Dr. Prouty, in a moment of morbid query, wondered what hash and eggs tasted like the second time around.

It went on like that for a good ten minutes, and even when the contents of Hymie's stomach had clearly been displaced, he just kept right on retching.

Vinchetti asked the seemly question, "Hey, Doc? How can he keep puking like that?"

"Dry heaves, as one might say," Prouty replied. "The copper sulphate will remain active for hours; the stomach will continue to spasm whether there's food in it or not. All he's vomiting up now is latent bile."

"I *like* it!" Vinchetti barked.

"Latent bile," Tony remarked. "That's a doozy of a dessert."

"And would you look at the skinny bitch?" the boss added. "She looks knocked up!"

The two subjects shivered on the table, both their faces pinkened in exhaustion, Hymie still dry-heaving, and their open mouths still securely stapled together. Prouty had been right in his estimation: Darcy, in order to stay alive, had indeed consumed the entirety of Hymie's vomit, but in that absolutely massive transference of partially digested food, one had to consider the disparity of proportions. Hymie, a 300-pound glutton, and Darcy, a 90-pound crack-tart. Now her own stomach was surely stretched to its physical limit; hence, the effect left the rack-skinny girl with an abdomen so bloated she looked as though she were in her third trimester of pregnancy. It was an amazing sight.

"Okay, Doc. Time to get things goin' in the other direction."

Dr. Prouty administered the next injection of vomitive, this time to Darcy, and the desired effect was almost instantaneous due to her diminutive body weight. The show began again, Hymie now on the receiving end.

"They'll just keep going like that till they die," the doctor assured.

"Aaaaaack! Aaaaaack! Aaaaaack!" was the sound that Darcy made once she began heaving in earnest.

"Peachy," Tony said.

Vinchetti frowned. "Yeah, but its gettin' a little—a little. Hey, Doc, what's the word I'm lookin' for?"

"Wearisome?"

Vinchetti scratched his chin. "What's that mean?"

"Boring."

Vinchetti cracked his hands together. "*That's* the word! Come on, let's go into office, leave these two to puke themselves to death. You too, Doc. I wanna show you and Tony my latest vid."

"Aaaaaack! Aaaaaack! Aaaaaack!" Darcy seemed to reply as they left. Vinchetti led them out of the work room and down a few dank cinderblock halls. Muted shrieks could be heard from a number of closed doors, and from somewhere deeper in the block compound, the pit bulls were at work again. Vinchetti stopped and opened one door, stuck his head in. A woman blubbered in a voice scarcely human: "Please, no more, no more . . ."

"Hey, fellas, how's it going?" Vinchetti called in.

"Great, boss. This hosebag's really kickin' it up."

"Neat-o. Later." Vinchetti closed the door, leading on. "Paulie and Charlie're in there skinnin' the bitch who runs our massage parlors in Utica. She was takin' clients on the side." He shook his head a moment. "Fuckin'-A. Looked like Paulie was pulling down wallpaper."

"Cunt had it coming," Tony remarked.

"It's a good trick. When they're done skinnin' her, Logman comes in and fucks her to high heaven. Comes all over her whiles she's shakin' on the floor red as a beet."

"Cool," Tony said. "So what's this *new* vid you're talkin' about, boss?"

"Aw, it's great, Tony. You'll love it. Come on in."

Vinchetti's office looked typical for a man of his stature: rich paneling, a side bar, cherrywood furniture. Behind the desk, a dark portrait of his father loomed, overseeing all. Several televisions and a row of VCR's occupied the opposing wall. Vinchetti hit the PLAY button on a remote.

"Nice," Tony said, looking up at a screen. There, a exquisitely shaped female rump was poised, fine and white as alabaster. Elegant fingers slipped back, parting the buttocks to reveal a delicate rectum.

Vinchetti whistled. "How's that for an ass? Ain't that somethin'?"

"Sure is, boss. Fuckin' thing should hang in a museum," Tony remarked.

Next, on the screen, a greased erection appeared, and within seconds, the beautiful derriere was being fastidiously sodomized. Dr. Prouty watched from aside, fairly bored.

Vinchetti turned up the sound. "Stick me!" a woman's hot voice implored. "Stick me right in the ass! All the way in! *Hard!*"

The penis on-screen obliged.

"Thing is," Vinchetti went on. "See that cock? It ain't *my* cock, I can tell ya that. But the ass that it's goin' in and out of happens to belong to my wife."

Tony's face was already going pale as cream. Before he could reach into his jacket for his gun, Vinchetti had already drawn down on him with his own pistol. The room seemed to freeze, its only movement coming from the tv screen where the sodomy continued. Eventually the camera lens opened, enlarging the scene well enough to show Vinchetti's pert strawberry-blond wife bent over a vanity. The man sodomizing her was Tony.

"Boss," Tony grated, "you don't understand . . ."

"I understand that you've been butt-fuckin' my wife in my bedroom. What else I need to understand? See, I had Lunky put a camera in there after he put the one in the cash room that fingered Hymie."

Beads of sweat trickled on Tony's forehead. "She came onto me, boss—I swear. Said if I didn't do it, she'd tell you lies about me. I swear on my mother's grave, boss!"

Vinchetti upped the volume some more, and now his wife—between proddings—snickered, "Thank God you had the balls to put the make on me, Tony. Ain't no one else in this joint's got the balls to."

Tony paled further as Vinchetti kept the pistol aimed at his head.

"A woman's got needs, ya know?" her voice continued. "A woman needs a *cock* up her ass sometimes, not that little thing my husband's got. Christ, it feels like one of those little Vienna sausages."

Oh, dear, Dr. Prouty thought.

Vinchetti turned off the video.

"Come on, boss," Tony pleaded, having already urinated in his farcical white slacks. "It was just one of those things, ya know? I didn't mean nothin' by it."

"Sure, Tony, sure. And I don't mean nothin' by this . . ." He gave a curt nod to Dr. Prouty who immediately stepped up behind Tony and snapped him in the side of the neck with a Bush automatic injector full of tranquilizers.

Tony staggered a moment, then was unconscious before he hit the floor.

Vinchetti's wife had been previously "prepared." Naked, of course, she sat strapped to an examination chair, her pretty head belted back against the adjustable head rest. Terror sheened her impeccable white skin and jutted her breasts out like ripe peaches above the chest strap. Tony, too, had been strapped to a chair, though far less intricately.

"You're a genius, Doc, a friggin' genius!" Vinchetti complimented, rubbing his hands together.

Dr. Prouty rolled his eyes.

Neither victim could make much in the way of vocal protest, just grunts from Tony and raving whimpers from Vinchetti's wife. No,

their mouths had not been stapled together like Hymie and Darcy—
Vinchetti like variation. Instead . . .

Pretty proficient work, if I may say so myself, the doctor thought.

He'd run a half-inch-wide esophageal catheter down the throat
of Vinchetti's wife, after which he'd instigated what you might call
a stomach-pump in reverse. He'd also, quite skillfully, performed
a modified ileostomy on her upper-left abdomenal quardant. In
medical terms, the procedure (unlike the more familiar colostomy),
circumvented the mid-small-intestinal process (known as the
jejunum) through a surgically constructed stoma (or aperture) after
which the small intestine was severed at this proximal point and
stitched to the inside of the stoma. Dr. Prouty's modification,
however, bypassed this final step, and merely extricated the the
severed instestinal length.

In less-than-medical terms, he'd cut a slit in Mrs. Vinchetti's
belly, reeled out some gut, and snipped it.

He'd left the lower end of the intestine to dangle. The higher end
he'd stapled to Tony's lips via the McCrath Model SS40-C.

"Looks like a hose runnin' from her stomach to Tony's yap,"
Vinchetti observed.

"Yes, a . . . hose," Dr. Prouty offered, "from which chyme,
mucosa, and partially digested intestinal material will empty."

Another familiar Vinchetti chuckle. "The low-down prick likes
stickin' his dick into my wife's shit, let's see how he likes eatin' it,
huh?"

"Precisely."

"It's almost like you hooked her ass up to his mouth!"

"In a manner of speaking, that's correct, sir. However, I thought
you would enjoy a variation of that description. What I'm referring
too, of course, is my decision to transect the jejunum rather than, say,
the sigmoid colon."

"Huh?" Vicnhetti expressed his incomprehension.

"It's the *large* intestine that wilts the majority of moisture from the feces, sir. But severing the digestive tract at the jejunum will detour that effect."

Vinchetti's brow creased. "She's gonna shit in his mouth, right, Doc?"

"Yes, but with intestinal matter that hasn't been fully subjected to the complete digestive process. What voids into Tony's mouth will be essentially diarrhea."

Vinchetti cracked his hands yet again. "The Hershey Squirts! Neat-o!"

"Yes, sir," the doctor continued to elaborate, "and given my previous preparation of goat cheese, raw garlic, baked beans, and canned dog food, it should make for an interesting mix." (After the ileostomy, Dr. Prouty has emptied this mish-mash of ingredients into Mrs. Vinchetti's stomach through the esophageal tube by means of a surgical aspirator pump.)

Tony's mute face began to redden, as Mrs. Vinchetti's bowels began to move.

"He'll have to eat it," Prouty said, "or he'll drown."

The gray-pink length of intestine began to squirm. Muffled gargling could be heard, and Tony's cheeks billowed hugely at each blast of diarrhea..

"Gorgeous, Doc. You're a true star." Vinchetti patted Prouty on the back and led him out of the room.

Dr. Prouty tried to rein his enthusiasm, to control himself. "So, um, we're done now, sir?"

"With them two? Sure. We'll let Tony chug on that for a while before I have the boys feed 'em both to the pits."

Warm joy surged through Prouty's veins. "So then . . . I can go now?"

"Sure, Doc, you can go just like I promised—"

Prouty nearly squealed in delight.

"—after pigs can fly and fuckin' Santa Claus come down the chimney to hold my dick for me when I piss," Vinchetti finished.

"When bears wear funny hats and the pope shits in the woods."

Prouty's heart seemed to drop to the floor. He stood and stared. "But . . . sir. You said—"

"Yeah, I know, I said you could leave if you fucked Hymie in the ass and got your nut before Tony." Another slap on the back. "But there's one thing you gotta learn, paisan. My word ain't worth a tick on a dead dog's balls. Never trust a goombah slime-bag mafia fuck like me, Doc." Vinchetti walked on, belting laughter, but then he turned and winked. "Me, you, and that fancy stapler of yours? We're gonna have ourselves a *lot* of fun in the years to come. Later, Doc! Have a great day!"

Dr. Prouty watched his boss disappear down the hallway.

Oh, well. It could be worse. There was always the hook.

ABOUT THE AUTHOR

Edward Lee has authored close to 50 books in the field of horror; he specializes in hardcore fare. His most recent novels are LUCIFER'S LOTTERY and the Lovecraftian THE HAUNTER OF THE THRESHOLD. His movie HEADER was released on DVD by Synapse Film in June, 2009. Lee lives in Largo, Florida.

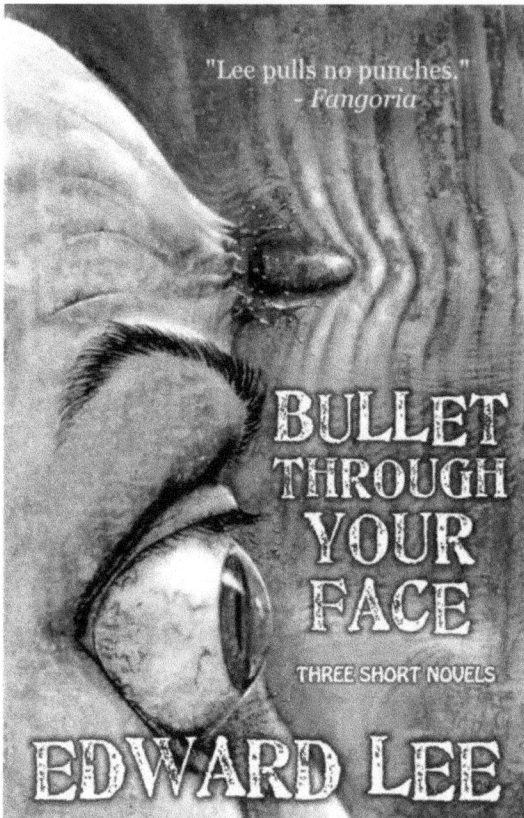

"Squid Pulp Blues" Jordan Krall - In these three bizarro-noir novellas, the reader is thrown into a world of murderers, drugs made from squid parts, deformed gun-toting veterans, and a mischievous apocalyptic donkey.

". . . with SQUID PULP BLUES, [Krall] created a wholly unique terrascape of Ibsen-like naturalism and morbidity; an extravaganza of white-trash urban/noir horror."
- Edward Lee

"Apeshit" Carlton Mellick III - Friday the 13th meets Visitor Q. Six hipster teens go to a cabin in the woods inhabited by a deformed killer. An incredibly fucked-up parody of B-horror movies with a bizarro slant

"The new gold standard in unstoppable fetus-fucking killfreakomania . . . Genuine all-meat hardcore horror meets unadulterated Bizarro brainwarp strangeness. The results are beyond jaw-dropping, and fill me with pure, unforgivable joy." - John Skipp

"Super Fetus" Adam Pepper - Try to abort this fetus and he'll kick your ass!

"The story of a self-aware fetus whose morally bankrupt mother is desperately trying to abort him. This darkly humorous novella will surely appall and upset a sizable percentage of people who read it... In-your-face, allegorical social commentary."
- BarnesandNoble.com

"Fistful of Feet" Jordan Krall -   A bizarro tribute to Spaghetti westerns, Featuring Cthulhu-worshipping Indians, a woman with four feet, a Giallo-esque serial killer, a crazed gunman who is obsessed with sucking on candy, Syphilis-ridden mutants, ass juice, burping pistols, sexually transmitted tattoos, and a house devoted to the freakiest fetishes.

"Krall has quite a flair for outrage as an art form."
- Edward Lee

www.ingramcontent.com/pod-product-compliance
Ingram Content Group UK Ltd.
Pitfield, Milton Keynes, MK11 3LW, UK
UKHW040641060525
5779UKWH00030B/193